50 Shades
of NATURAL Gray

Spicy Stories
for the
Seasoned Woman

Eve Publishing, Rockwood, ON Canada
Editors: Marcia Zina Mager, Alberta Nye, Gloria Nye

Published by Eve Publishing,
 8178 Indian Trail,
 Rockwood, ON N0B 2K0
Canada

www.evepublishing.com

evepublishing@gmail.com

The food poems in shaded boxes were written by Alberta Nye

ISBN 978-0-9919798-3-7

50 Shades
of NATURAL Gray

Spicy Stories
for the
Seasoned Woman

Eve Publishing

"I've always been attracted to women who are assertive and have confidence - qualities older women possess. They've been on the Earth a little longer. They're more seasoned. They don't play games. They know what they want, and they're not afraid to tell you."

Taye Diggs

Table of Contents

"Sleeping with a man half your age can be exhausting, but if it's too much for him you can always find a younger man."

Barbara Taylor Bradford

Introduction

Forever Young

Getting older is quite a trip. I remember looking in the mirror when I was about 40 years old and discovering my first gray hairs. It rocked my world. *Who needs hallucinogenic drugs, I thought, when you've got this wild can't-ever-get-off roller coaster ride called aging.* No matter what we do, no matter what we eat, no matter how much we exercise or pray or chant affirmations, we all continue to age, to get wrinkles; we all march, every day, toward the conclusion of this intense and magnificent and mysterious thing called Life.

But here's the kicker. Here's the unbelievable, miraculous, can-I-get-a-witness gospel song. Inside, inside, we are young. That never ever changes. There is an invisible eternity, a pure, clear, infinite wellspring in each of us, even if it doesn't seem to match the wrinkled neck, sagging cheeks, and aging hands.

So that brings me to the edgy subject of sex. Well, maybe sex itself isn't all that edgy, but sex for those of us over 50, over 60, over 70, over 80 seems to cause all kinds of reactions. Especially if the older woman is not that sort of drop dead still-gorgeous Helen Mirren type. You know, the woman who doesn't look her age (at least in the air brushed magazine ads). The woman who has "aged well" and who the public might be more willing to consider a sexual being without rolling their eyes, smirking, or wrinkling their noses in disgust.

Yet the bottom line is that sexuality, sensuality, juiciness, eroticism, and orgasm is still part of all of us no matter how our outer body changes. Oh, sure, it might get repressed, shoved aside, ignored, dismissed, denied. But that doesn't mean it's not there, deep inside, waiting, brewing, stewing, steaming, and steeping in its own life-affirming juice.

Because inside, inside we are forever young.

That's why we at Eve Publishing wanted to acknowledge and applaud (our) seasoned sexuality. Yes, the millions of silver haired damsels (dyed or not) who still have outrageous erotic fantasies, real-life affairs, actual orgasms, and all other sorts of sexy, sundry, sassy, feisty, feverish, fierce, brazen, brash, and bold experiences. Our sincere wish in publishing *50 Shades of Natural Gray* is to celebrate the juicy vitality brimming in older women—our sizzle, our hunger, our wild fantasy lives, and yes, our grip-the-sheets-point-the-toes-arch-the-back indisputable, unadulterated orgasms.

The moral of this, uh, immoral story? Heat doesn't just belong to the sizzling slender twenty-something Anastasias of the world. It belongs to us, too. Move over, Christian Grey, because we're a'comin.

Marcia Zina Mager
Editor
Eve Publishing

Erica Jong was Right
Leslie Hobson

Hey Birdie~

Sorry I haven't written or called for a while. It's one of those nights where I really wish you weren't halfway around the world. If it wouldn't disrupt your entire household I would probably call you right now.

This is one of those emails that you are going to have to delete. Burn after Reading kind of thing. Delete it and then delete it again from your trash—promise? I have got to tell somebody what happened tonight and you are the only one I trust. So here goes.

I was out tonight. Not out in the way you have been pushing. I was at my Book Club. Yes, with a bunch of other middle aged women. Well at least it's a start. You really don't seem to get that after being married for 21 years doing stuff on my own is still hard.

This Book Club is a big step for me. A woman at work asked me to join and she is the only one there that I know. The first two went really well but this month it was that stupid *Fifty Shades* book. I actually hadn't read it but thought I could get through the meeting with what I have picked up hearing about it. God knows everyone has been talking about it!

But it went way over the top. Some of these women were able to talk about things that, seriously, I could never say to anyone but you—really personal stuff about their husbands, or some old boyfriend, or some guy at the gym. Wow. When it was my turn, I said that I had been married for 21 years to a Certified General Accountant. They all nodded so I could pretty much leave it at that.

I didn't bother to tell them that he left me for a junior accountant at his firm. (*"Figures,"* was what you said at the time. Remember? And then *"Sorry, too soon?"*) I also didn't mention that I hadn't been with anyone else since he left. Do you know that it's coming on 4 years? Jesus. Time flies whether you are having fun or not.

So I'm sitting there, feeling embarrassed while they are sharing these stories and maybe I drank a little more wine that I should have. I think we all did. The conversation got quite wild and while it was mostly pretty funny, I was actually starting to feel more than a little turned on by some of their stories.

It was almost 11:00 when we finally broke up. When I got into the car I remembered my fuel warning light had gone on the way to the meeting. Now I had the long drive home and wasn't sure I was going to make it without stopping for gas so I kept my eye out for an all-night station.

I saw one just off the highway and pulled off. When it took me a couple of tries to get my credit card into the slot I knew that I probably shouldn't have been driving. But there was no traffic, just a lovely clear night with the cool breeze washing away the heat of the day.

The only other vehicle at the station was a pickup truck.

One of those super-sized black ones that looks like it's on steroids. The man who walked around from the far side of the truck took my breathe away. Literally. I think he heard me gasp.

I'm not sure exactly what it was about him. He just was so . . . male. Probably about 40, maybe more, tanned and rough looking in the best way. His clothes were clean but he looked like he worked outside. He also looked like he could snap my ex-husband like a twig.

So he glances over at me and I am totally staring at him. Not even surreptitiously. I am *gaping* at him. Good lord. I turn around really fast and start filling my tank. But I can't help myself. I look back at him over my shoulder. He's still looking at me and now he's smiling.

Bird, I don't know what the hell I was thinking, but I smiled at him. Not a '*have a nice day*' smile, but a real, come hither kind of '*yeah that's right I'm looking at you*' smile. I kept looking at him and smiling and damn if he didn't start walking over towards me.

I didn't know what to do. I was breathing fast and could feel my heart pounding. I turned my back to him and kept filling my tank. When I glanced back again he was standing ***right there***. Right behind me. He had his head cocked and his arms crossed and that damn smile.

I took a deep breath and finished with the gas. Turned and put the nozzle back into the pump. Now we were both hidden from the clerk in the booth by the pumps. And he was so close that I could reach out and touch him. So I did.

I honestly don't know what I was thinking. I just reached out my hand and ran my middle finger down his chest, from the hair curling out at the top of his plaid work shirt, right down to the buckle on his belt. Then I leaned back against my car and waited to see what he would do.

Slowly, really slowly, he moved up to me and slipped one hand behind me to the small of my back. He leaned in until his thigh was pressed between my legs. He was so much bigger than me. He leaned way down and put his mouth on my neck. Not kissing, or licking, just . . . contact. Just moving his mouth down my neck to my collarbone. I could feel his breath.

At the same time he slid his other hand down between my legs and cupped me. He just started moving his fingers slightly, just a smooth, constant pulsing as he pushed his fingers against my thin silk pants. He pulled harder against my back so I was being moved between his two hands and kind of riding on his leg at the same time. It only went on for a couple of minutes and I began to pant and push myself against him.

I threw my head back and I came. Hard. And loud. Oh, my God! He held on to me in the same way—still outside of my clothes—until I stopped shaking. And then he kissed me. Just once. On the cheek. He smiled again and winked at me, and sort of nodded. Then he turned around and walked back to his truck, started the engine and drove away.

I caught my breath, got in my car and drove home. That's it. It really happened. Wild, right? We didn't actually . . . you know. But it was truly zipless. Erica Jong was right.

I came for sex
Quiverdance

standing before me
you barely touched me with your hands
instead you closed your eyes
and drew your breath
drawing all my shivering desires
inside your soul

I felt them go
your gentle touch knows
senses what I feel now
your breath on my neck
seduces me, inhales me
takes what I'll give willingly
demands the rest
slides me under into your world

I thought I came for sex
but I got it wrong
sex came for me
in your eyes, in your fingertips
maybe on our maiden voyage sex came first
but now
when I feel you breathing
I come for you.

ALMOND

The almond is a symbol
Of fertility it's said.
Arousing female passion,
So keep some by your bed.

Aromas prod the senses
And almond is so strong.
Inhale deeply as you lie,
While it sings its sensual song!

Mystery
Eve Milan

Vivienne's hand shook as she unlocked the door. At seven in the morning, the office was fairly dark and she fumbled with the cord on the Tiffany lamp while juggling a Mocha Latte Grande and her one total indulgence, a cinnamon croissant.

A small black lacquer box sat prominently on her desk. Considering that the office was locked, how it got there was not only a curiosity, but a bold new twist in a delicate contest of wills. Chinese-red letters carved into the side of the box taunted her with the one word—*Mystery*.

As soon as she saw the shiny box, she knew the control over her plans for her day had been blasted to smithereens. As curious as she was about this box, her eyes were drawn to the window.

He was there. Standing in the window in the building across the street. Watching. Her. Her office window had Victorian lace curtains. It was the only window in the entire building with curtains. Perhaps it was this anomaly that had originally caught his mischievous attention thirty-nine days ago.

Pretending to ignore his watchful eyes, she slid into her ergonomic chair and stared at the small box. The more she studied it, the larger it became, until it filled every inch of her mental horizon. She could almost hear this box scream as if it had a soul waiting to be released. Vivienne didn't want to touch it and she fought her fierce curiosity, especially since he was watching her.

Without saying a word, he had changed the rules of the game by entering her space. How had he done it? She flashed on a wiry thought. Had he ever been inside her office before? Clearly today, a boundary had been crossed. It melted the rules of whatever she could be sure she knew. It felt like the ocean pulling away the sand from her toes. With this simple act— entering her private space—he had changed the unwritten rules. He has entered her world. Vivienne had always seen herself as a creature of habit, but he had found an invisible string to pull, and all she could do was watch herself unravel.

In one way it felt liberating. She was not some young blushing princess, and part of her wanted him to break down her self-imposed castle walls. But in the next moment, a flicker of violation tugged at her, the dangerous awareness that he was leading her with the distant force of his focused intention.

She took a sip of the coffee, hoping to settle herself, but the sharp ring of the phone made her jump. Hot coffee streaked over her fingers and she stifled a response to the sudden pain. She turned away from the phone to stare out her seventeenth floor window.

She watched him slide his Bluetooth over his ear beneath his dark hair and raise his binoculars. He had explained to her in explicit, loving detail all about his prized Helios PNB-2 Russian Border Guard 110 mm binoculars. Once intended for long range observation of targets and determination of their angular coordinates, they now found a softer use. He had, however, been vague about his eleven years as an Air Force pilot, claiming his missions were routine, (which made her fairly certain they were anything but). One thing was certain, he clearly had the discipline of a patient observer. Apparently she had Uncle Sam to thank for his being so thoroughly equipped to stalk his prey.

She continued to ignore the ringing phone, although she knew she would answer. If she didn't answer, he would just leave his usual one-word message on her voice mail. He would say they were just words that felt nice in his mouth at the moment, but those odd words, spoken in his deeply resonant tones, would haunt her all day as she searched for possible deeper layers of hidden meaning. He once left a message with just the word *adagio* and another time, *shimmer,* and another time, *cupcake.*

Those words played on her lips all day. Vivienne reached for the phone. She didn't want to spend another sleepless night ruminating on the meaning of one of his one-word messages.

"How did you get inside my. . ."

"Open it." He said. His voice licked at her.

The sonorous, now so familiar sound, softened her lips into a girlish grin. His lazy, commanding coolness filled her. He was training her in the art of letting him have his way. As a token of obedience, she picked up the box, which was smaller than her hand. She could see inside the glass cover to the round antique bottle within and those red *Mystery* letters. It cost one hundred and ninety-five dollars for an ounce of this Turkish fragrance laced with exotic bergamot. She knew because she had priced it on an obscure perfume website the day he told her it was his favorite scent. She was more than curious to fill her olfactory senses, but in his own twisted way, he was teaching her to savor the wait. She didn't open the bottle to release the fragrance.

"Put it on."

She ignored his instruction. Giving in too soon would reduce the sensation he was carefully evoking. Vivienne would have never described herself as patient. Now she had a growing greed for maximizing the pleasure that comes from the *art* of delayed gratification.

"The *mystery* is how you got it on to my desk."

Vivienne picked up her demure mother-of-pearl opera glasses and peered back at him. She smiled on the inside, delighted with her small deception that he assumed his viewing power was so much greater than hers. Knowing about his military background, it tickled her that he didn't have a clue that she had spent four-hundred dollars replacing the original lenses in her dainty opera glasses with high-powered Zeiss optics. She would never tell him. Why should he know how many details she could see? Or how much she had paid to see them.

"This is a secure building," she said. "I lock my door when I leave at night so I can't imagine how you got in."

Vivienne assumed her slight tilt of the opera glasses to scan his body wasn't obvious. She had practiced making this subtle move at her bathroom mirror and now made this sly movement safely, scanning his perfectly pressed light blue shirt. Last week she had commented on the quality of his shirts, and he had told her about his tailor in Thailand, who made them precisely sized for him. Huge, the way the few details she knew so completely, contrasted with the volumes of unknowns about this man. She glanced at the monogrammed initials on the cuffs, subtly sewn in silk thread two shades darker.

"The power of big tipping," he replied. He paused, giving her eyes time to linger. "It opens many doors in life."

"I see. Just how big was it?"

"The cleaning man let me know it would have to be sizable for him to risk losing his job. Don't worry, I didn't snoop. He stood there the whole time, while I placed it on your desk."

Curious, the tiny things he took the time to reassure her about, considering he was such a master at unhinging everything she had come to take for granted about herself. Such as what a shy girl he assumed she was. She was certainly not the kind of woman to come to work two hours early to stare across the street at a man she'd never met. Or the kind of woman who would give her phone number to a stranger. Or . . . let a man touch secret spots in her mind.

She remembered the day, twenty-nine days ago when he had gotten her to give him her phone number. He pretended to hold a phone to his ear. Then he held up one finger at a time, waiting for her nod to indicate each correct gesture, until he had deciphered her seven digit phone number. Of course he tried it immediately. She liked that he was clever and that he could turn the simplest communication into an intriguing game. This game was not like any she had ever played before. In *his* game it was never clear who was winning. It was unpredictable and chipped away at her old image of who she was. Following his lead meant finding out what she was capable of, and discovering what she might do next.

"Put it on."

"It" being *your* scent?"

"In a moment it's going to be your scent. Put it on."

"Why? Do your Helios PNB-2's possess the sense of smell? Or are you planning to stage our first face-to-face encounter?"

These last words were a challenge. They startled her as much as they seemed to him. She hadn't planned them. Rather she heard them coming fresh out of her mouth just as he did. There was no calling them back. He was a genius at getting her to surprise herself. She watched his weight shift. He was silent, but by now she could feel the nuances in his silence. It was sublime that her idea had so stirred him. She loved these micro-moments between them, where the balance of power tipped completely. If only for a second.

"Because I want to be in control of your scent," he replied. He was ignoring the real challenge she had posed.

Vivienne listened to the slight change in his breathing. She had been denied the intoxication of experiencing his touch, and was highly attuned to the resonant undulations of his baritone voice. And it was oh so much fun that just a few provocative, unanticipated words from her lips could startle and ignite him. The delicious power made her tingle.

She particularly liked the potent silences she could tease out between them. It gave her time to study him. Even at this distance she could sense his arms were strong and toned. He had described his eyes as "a lonely shade of blue." When she looked into them, face to face, would she be able to see the black hole of loneliness? She had a feeling they would ignite everything they landed on. She wondered if they could burn through her fear.

And she wondered how it would feel to have her fingers wander through his black hair, pulling just slightly when he wasn't expecting it? Would his breath feel warm, grazing against her cheek? Would her brain be intoxicated by his musky pheromones? She had imagined all these first moments many times.

But she didn't want to risk making them real, where they could become less than her perfect movie of the mind. The one place where she had control of him was in her mind and it was too high a price to give that up for immutable reality.

"I like your butterfly," he said.

"What?"

He had this way of roller coasting her brain, making her feel like she was always catching up.

"The one fluttering around your lovely neck."

Vivienne looked down. She had put on that necklace that morning, just for him and the scoop neck blouse that she knew would command his eyes. She had won the emerald and gold necklace in a High School essay contest and been so proud the day she'd received it at age seventeen. And yet somehow it had spent 30 years sleeping in its original box. Then one day, after he told her of his fondness for butterflies, she had spent hours, searching for it through boxed memories.

"Did you wear it just for me?" he asked, penetrating her private ruminations.

"No," she lied. And wondered why she lied.

"I think you did."

Caught! Feeling cornered, her primal brain sent impulses to run but her rational brain overruled. After all, how absurd it would be to run out of your own office.

"You said you liked butterflies. So, I . . ." Such a tiny

admission, but she felt like she had just surrendered the Alamo. "I have to go. I have work to do. I'm going to hang up now."

"No, you won't."

"Watch me!" Vivienne said, taking a small step away from the lace curtain. "Pun intended!"

"I'll just call you back."

"I won't answer."

"Yes, you will."

"How do you know that?"

"For the same reason you haven't hung up already."

Ouch. "Don't you have work to do?" she taunted.

"I've already done nine-hundred thousand in trades for my Tokyo Twins. Bratty little rich kids. Eleven years old and their combined portfolio is bigger than my boss's. I deserve a coffee break. Another Grande Mocha Latte . . . sweetened with you. And your . . . *Mystery*."

"I'm busy."

They both laughed. The little giddy laugh that accompanies the flash of self awareness. The mini-moment of truth where you remember what you're really doing. Which in Vivienne's case was standing in her office window on the seventeenth floor at 7:25 in the morning, holding a pair of souped-up opera glasses and staring at a stranger across the street.

He was so inescapably close. So achingly far. They had so perfected this simultaneous tease.

Not even a fire drill would make them turn away. She could see him lowering his binoculars to scan her body. He never tried to be subtle.

"What are you looking at?

Silence.

He never bothered to answer a question that didn't leave him in command.

"Say something."

"Put on the *Mystery.*

"I can't. Not now. I have to get these revisions done. We have a meeting with the clients …"

"That's not until eleven," he interrupted, flummoxing her brain again.

"Huh? How do you know that?"

"'Davis—Revisions 11AM.' Post-it note on your screen."

Vivienne looked back at her computer. There it was, on a heart-shaped pink post-it-note.

"You can read my post-its? That's just way too . . ."

"*Intimate.*"

"I can't believe you read my post-it notes. That's way too . . . personal."

She furtively scanned the room for other things he might know that she didn't know he knew. Telltale signs of how important this stranger from across the skyscraper had become. Unlike his immaculate and pristine office with nothing revealing or personal out of place, her small office looked like a Victorian tea party had exploded. One wall held a crammed bulletin board with fliers and notices for events she would never get around to attending. An antique feathered hat sat on top of a filing cabinet, and a pair of long red velvet gloves draped over her bookshelf lay next to two Queen Ann tea cups. A framed Renoir print of a dancing couple with a lady in a long white ruffled dress hung on her door. Every cozy inch was filled with animal figurines and all kinds of sweet and idyllic images that might inspire her in her job of writing text for customized greeting cards—and to protect her from the ugliness of ordinary life.

"Don't worry. I've read everything. There's nothing very interesting."

"Should that be a relief? How is it you always catch me with my hand in your cookie jar?"

"Except that blue post-it. Who is 'Mario @ 7'?"

She quickly searched and found the blue post-it perched on her cuckoo clock.

"Carlos. My Rhumba teacher."

"Rhumba. I see. That adds an intriguing new dimension to my lady in the lace window. How is your Cuban Motion?"

She blushed at the mention of the sensuous hip motion—surprised he knew the technical term.

"Do you dance?" she asked, hoping she had sufficiently disguised the excitement she imagined dancing with him.

"Better than Carlos, I'm sure."

"Oh, really? Carlos won the Latin-American Championship at Cherry Hill." She was delighted to fan a flicker of jealousy at the other end of the phone.

"What year?" he shot back.

Ouch.

"1987," she admitted. "Where did you learn to dance? Did you take the Arthur Murray special crash course for spies?"

"Two years stationed in Latin America. I wouldn't have survived if I couldn't dance. You can fire Carlos. Tonight."

She laughed at how serious he sounded. "Carlos is very patient with me. He has another student who is a former nun. Put it this way, she's better than I am. You know. With all those Cuban—."

"Hips. I'm not sure I like the idea of another man being close enough to inhale your . . . *Mystery*."

She took a deep breath, "If you were brave enough to put less than a street between us, *you* could be the one doing the inhaling."

Silence on his end. He lowered his binoculars. Today was the first time she had challenged him with a direct invitation. The first time *she* had upped the rules of this game.

Thirty-nine days of window-to-window teasing. The longing and frustration had become the perfect companion. She was confident he wasn't going to ruin the magnificent imagining by making it real.

"What?" he said.

Suddenly she couldn't think of an answer to W*hat?*

After a very long time, he said, "Okay."

"Okay . . . *what?*"

"Okay. I'm coming over."

"Now? Here? That's not a good idea!" Fear and fire mixed, combusting inside her.

"It was your idea."

"Yeah, but I think the first time we meet in person should be like a real . . . date."

"What's a real date?"

"In a restaurant. Or at the Opera. A gallery opening. I don't know."

"Nobody knows what the perfect first meeting is."

"Yes, but we should plan something."

"You plan something and it can all blow up in a thousand ways."

"You think it will . . .blow up?" Vivienne twisted and tormented a strand of hair, convinced that he had already decided it would. There was a long silence.

"Tell you what. Let's not plan anything."

"But, I need to . . .prepare."

"Just put on the *Mystery*.

And he hung up the phone.

She watched him carefully put the Russian Border Guard binoculars down on his desk. She watched him slowly straighten his silk tie and put on his dark blue Armani jacket. She watched him leave his office on the seventeenth floor across the street and close the door.

Then the raw truth hit her. He's coming over.

The sheltered, tantalizing tender *Mystery* was about to be subjected to the unpredictable ravages of reality.

Her heart leapt over the moon.

Sunday, I want to get religious with you
Mary Ann Moore

This poem previously appeared in *You Are Here*,
Poems by Mary Ann Moore (Leaf Press, 2012)

The waning light, you across the room.
On the Persian carpet, its memories of Rumi's *gulistan*,
the cat stretches in *savasana,*
legs splayed, a soft surrender there.

I peel an orange, fingers penetrating the pungent flesh,
mouthing each part from the palm of my hand.
Delight at the tang on my tongue, the splash of juice
as I bite. The slow, languorous swallow.

Glancing up from your reading, you catch my eye,
then my finger as I suck the shaft of it.

The need to shorten the distance, urgent.
Can only think of orange with deep red beets,
pomegranate seeds, garlic that swells as it warms.
The taste of you
after you've tasted me.

FIG

The fig you say?
A sexy fruit? This tiny withered thing?
It hardly is a vision
that makes my hormones sing.

The leaves have worked in ancient times
To cover private places.
T'was Cleopatra's favourite fruit,
She ate them by the cases.

Ancient Greeks connected them
To love and to fertility.
They held them up as sacred things
To augment their ability.

So who am I to criticize
This lowly little fruit?
I have more wrinkles than it does
And I don't give a hoot.

I'm still moist and juicy too
And wont to take a lover.
A lesson I have therefore learned
"Don't judge it by its cover."

To Live Again
Annabel Sheila

Grief consumed every waking moment and it was slowly destroying me. I was turning into someone I didn't recognize anymore. The unbelievable pain was deeply physical and emotional and I'd begun to wonder if I'd ever recover. There was nowhere to hide from the smothering blackness that shrouded my pitiful existence.

Gregory had passed away six months earlier and life as I knew it was over. How could I go on without him? He'd been my first and I promised him he'd be my last. Now in my late sixties, I had no family to call my own. I was angry with him that he died so suddenly, leaving me alone after forty years together, but in my heart I knew anger toward him wasn't reasonable. However, it was the only way I could deal with the pain.

My best friend Lynn suggested a vacation in Mexico might be just what I needed to lift me out of the black hole I'd buried myself in. Tearfully, she told me she was concerned that if I stayed on the self-destructive path I was on, grief was going to take me away from her and she couldn't bear the thought of losing me.

My husband and I had been travelling to Mexico every winter for years and it I was hesitant to go without him because the loneliness would be even more unbearable in the beautiful country where we'd spent so many happy times.

I'll never forget the day she dragged me into the travel agency where I reluctantly booked the trip. Surprisingly, it had felt good to put on make-up that morning and shed my grey sweats pants and T-shirt.

It was a warm spring day and we went for lunch first. I couldn't believe how much better I felt just getting out of the house. Lynn and I discussed selling my place when I returned from my trip. A large four bedroom bungalow filled to the rafters with memories made it far too easy to get lost in the past.

I've thanked her a thousand times since that day, because she forced me to realize Gregory was the one who had died, not me. And at the rate I'd been going, I probably would have joined him in a very short time.

As I packed away Gregory's things and prepared for the trip, I found myself, oddly enough, looking forward to the change of scenery and the relaxed camaraderie one finds in tropical destinations. I would be travelling with a group of sixty-something year olds so the odds were some of them might be widows. It might be comforting to share experiences with someone who'd understand what it's like to be left alone after a lifetime of being a couple.

The day of departure arrived, and my nerves were shattered. But, after making sure I had her contact information tucked into my handbag, just in case, Lynn gave me a reassuring hug and sent me off.

As the jet raced down the runway, the grief and misery of the past six months began to pull away from me, like I was leaving a ton of baggage behind. I felt both elated and a little gloomy. Memories of Mexico included Gregory and although I knew it would be upsetting once we landed, I felt determined to at least try. For far too long I'd merely existed.

The gentleman and his wife seated next to me were making the trip for their 50th wedding anniversary and excitedly informed me it was their maiden voyage to Mexico. They asked if I were travelling alone and when I explained, they fell all over themselves apologizing until I assured them I was fine and had decided to move on. In truth, I felt more than a little gloomy at their obvious happiness together but mostly because Gregory and I would never get to celebrate our 50th. Their kindness and compassion toward a virtual stranger was heartwarming.

They had a million questions about Mexico and the places I'd been and what they should see. Their plan was to stay in Cancun one week for the celebration, and then move on to the Mayan Riviera. Since we had stayed in pretty much every nook and cranny in the country, I was able to offer them in depth knowledge that few travel agents have. I found myself sharing experiences they were delighted to hear about and laughing for the first time in six months.

We sipped complimentary drinks and chatted for the duration of the flight and promised to keep in touch once we reached our destination. They even invited me to their hotel for the celebration that would include family members flying in from all over Canada. It felt good to be among the living again.

Once we were settled into the resort, I immediately booked a shopping trip into town the next day. I didn't bring much clothing with me as I planned to spend my time alone, reading and enjoying the beach. One suitcase with a few bathing

suits, shorts, skirts and a casual dress for dinner was all I'd
brought. A new dress was in order, and it would have to be at
least somewhat formal, for I had every intention of attending the
event that might prove to be the highlight of my trip.

All things considered, I still looked pretty good for my
age. My natural blonde shoulder length hair had become streaked
with silver lights over the years, but I'd taken pains to protect my
skin and had few wrinkles. I still had a pretty good figure too,
but clothes had been the last thing on my mind, and since
Gregory passed I was at least two sizes smaller. The time had
come to refresh my wardrobe and the designer shops on the strip
in Cancun were going to be the salvation of a weary widow's
panache and a definite boost to her ego.

Gregory and I had a good life together, and throughout our
years of wedded bliss we'd accumulated a nest egg for our
retirement. We planned to travel until our health wouldn't allow
it. But he'd scarcely turned sixty-five when a brain aneurysm
took him without warning. Now I began thinking that maybe I'd
follow through with our plan, albeit alone.

The next morning I awoke to a glorious dawn. Stepping
onto the freshly painted balcony of my sixth floor suite, I took in
the magnificent blue-green sea, heavenly scent of flowers on the
balmy breeze and the sounds of hotel carts moving quietly about
the resort as the staff prepared for the new day. My thoughts
drifted to happier times. God how I missed him! We'd shared so
many dawns exactly like this one, leisurely sipping our coffees
on the balcony while we planned our next adventure before
joining the early risers for breakfast at the buffet.

The melancholy mood threatened to disarm me of the

resolve to move forward, so shrugging off a heavy shawl of grief I stepped back inside to get dressed. The bus would be coming by around nine and there was no way I was going to miss it. But at that moment it wouldn't have taken much for me to crawl into the king-sized bed and wallow in misery.

I slipped into a little white cotton sundress that clung to every contour, and added a pair of red sandals. Then I brushed my hair until it gleamed, considered pulling it into a ponytail but chose instead to let it fall to my shoulders. A touch of lipstick and a quick glance in the mirror left me with a wide grin as a morbid thought crossed my mind. I didn't look half bad for a woman who had pretty much recently risen from the dead.

A number of male heads turned when I entered the dining room, leaving me feeling vibrantly alive. The attention was exciting, and after a light breakfast with two cups of strong black coffee I was raring to go.

When the bus arrived there were seats for only half of the passengers so I stood in the center aisle, gripping the well-worn overhead steel rail. My pale skin, blonde hair and grey-blue eyes were a sharp contrast to the locals on their way to work. They probably wondered why I chose this method of travel when there were plenty of reasonably priced, air-conditioned taxis available to take guests wherever they wanted. But Gregory and I always travelled by bus whenever we visited Mexico, so we could mingle and get a feel for the beautiful country. In fact, during the last couple of years, we avoided the resorts altogether, choosing instead to stay in the colorful little villages. Our trips became far more memorable and the warmth and hospitality of the Mexican people was amazing. They treated us like family and we made friends with people who invited us into their homes every time we returned.

A tall young man, perhaps in his late twenties, early thirties, with rich ebony eyes stood facing me. His hard, muscular body rubbed against mine every time the bus hit a bump. I tried not to stare, but he was breathtaking. Perfectly chiseled features with a clean, fresh look, he oozed masculinity. He wore a crisp white short-sleeved shirt that caressed strong biceps and hung loosely over tightly fitting blue jeans. The first three buttons of his shirt were undone, exposing a warm brown chest with dark hair scattered sparsely across it. And he smelled like heaven.

A sultry breeze off the sparkling turquoise ocean drifted in the open windows, stroking every inch of me with a sensual heat. His thighs brushed against mine as the crowded bus pressed us closer together. The firmly toned body that was surely sculpted by the gods was turning my insides into mush.

His dark eyes held mine, like he was soul searching, and my breathing became ragged. My body had a will of its own and the urge to taste his lips and abandon myself to the surprising passion stirring within me was overwhelming. Imagination ran rampant. He couldn't possibly be interested in me. For heaven's sakes, he was half my age. We hadn't spoken a single word, and yet something extraordinary was happening between us. The blood coursing through my veins grew red hot.

The bus swerved around a car parked beside the road, throwing me against his delicious torso. He reached out and held me firmly against him to keep me from falling. The heat was so intense I felt myself flush to the roots of my hair. The soft hair on his chest drew my gaze as tiny droplets of sweat lingering there teased my senses. His male scent was intoxicating.

Trying to maintain some semblance of control, I smiled and nodded thanks. He grinned, exposing perfect teeth, and in his fathomless eyes I saw us together on a pristine sandy beach, naked bodies drenched in the heat of passion, writhing with insatiable craving beneath a brilliant azure sky. I was practically panting now. The fantasy of spring mingling with autumn was eroding every sensibility I possessed.

Oh my God! What was wrong with me? That deliciously tingly feeling deep inside was something I thought I'd never feel again. And yet in a foreign country on a crowded bus I found myself fantasizing about a complete stranger.

There was no tension in the silence between us, but the sexual electricity, at least for me, was scorching. Every inch of me felt alive as my hardened nipples strained against the light cotton fabric of my dress, now drenched with moisture.

When we reached a little neighborhood on the outskirts of the shopping district, the bus came to an abrupt stop. Our bodies pressed tightly together one last time. Resistance was futile and I melted into him. Once again he held me while gripping the overhead rail to steady us both. With our faces scant inches apart, he gave me a deep searching look before slowly dropping his arm to his side.

I had the overpowering urge to close my eyes, because in the fantasy he was about to press his mouth against mine. I was caught in a raging inferno. The crowd milled forward to the exit, carrying him along with them and he disappeared. I slid onto the nearest seat, certain my shaky legs wouldn't hold me up a minute longer. Then I moved to the open window where a light breeze drifted into the steamy interior of the almost deserted bus. I felt so alive it was all I could do not to shout it out. Maybe I could be happy again. At least I knew for sure I wanted to live again. With my heart pounding wildly, I resisted the insane urge to rush after him.

The intimacy we'd shared, at least in my fantasy, had clouded every ounce of decorum I possessed and in that moment I would have followed him to the ends of the earth or made love to him right there on the street if he wanted to. But I closed my eyes and drew a deep shaky breath. What had I been thinking?

I hadn't felt that kind of wildly abandoned desire in eons. Now, at sixty-six, I joyfully realized life was far from over. I was a widow yes, but still capable of great passion. And I needed to feel that ancient heat between a man and a woman again. I loved Gregory with every fiber of my being and would have remained faithful to him forever. However I realized the passion we'd shared in our earlier years had been missing long before death took him. We were best friends and we shared everything, but we rarely made love anymore and it had left me feeling less than desirable. In fact, I thought he'd lost interest in me sexually and I'd practically given up on the intimate side of our marriage.

The time for grieving was done. I needed to embrace new friendships, enjoy fresh experiences and maybe even find someone wonderful to share my life with. At the very least I wanted to have sex again.

The bus began to move away and I saw my secret lover scoop a laughing little girl with eyes just like his into his arms. A beautiful young woman with long black waist length hair and a body that would stop traffic tucked her arm possessively into his.

He glanced over his shoulder, searching the bus until our eyes met. Then with a nearly imperceptible nod, he walked away and I knew I was going to be all right. A chapter in life had ended, but the story was far from over.

"Older women know who they are, and that makes them more beautiful than younger ones. I like to see a face with some character. I want to see lines. I want to see wrinkles. "

Naveen Andrews

LYCHEE NUT

The lychee nut is not a nut
But what then could it be?
A fruit that lurks within a crust
Waiting to be free.

So peel it back
And let your tongue
Explore the ins and outs
The thrill you feel is but a taste
Of lips that surely pout.

Other lips await your touch
Of tender tips and tongue
So practice on for what's to come
And your praises will be sung

Enjoy the taste and silky feel
For you'll find when you explore
The very same sensations
Will make her ask for more.

Love and Lust in the Canadian Wilderness

Excerpted from *Deer Eyes*,
a novel by Sonia Day

The plot: Shep, a Canadian airline pilot and deer hunter, and Adie, a botanical artist from New York, are would-be lovers whose road to romance is thwarted by complications. For starters, they're both married to other people. There's also been a misunderstanding about phone calls. Yet the attraction between them is powerful. Here, they meet by accident on a lonely country road, during a snowstorm.

"I don't believe it. It's YOU," she said.

"I don't believe it either," he said

"Jesus Christ, girl, why are you standing at the side of the road in weather like this?"

"I should think that's obvious, *boy.* You moron. I slid into the ditch. I didn't realize there'd be so much snow. I'm not used to . . . to driving in this kind of . . ." Snow flakes glistened on her lashes and her upper lip. She seemed about to cry. "I was hoping someone would stop and help me."

He strode forward and put his arms around her. She felt as cold and stiff as a popsicle on a stick. She was shivering. She leaned against his chest. Let him pull her close. Yet at the same time he sensed her reluctance, as if what she really wanted to do was pound the shit out of him.

"Look, Adie," he said, holding her back for a moment so he could look into her face. "Don't be mad, please. Let's get into my truck so you can warm up, at least. Then I'll explain everything."

Her teeth chattered as he led her over to the pickup.
The cab windows steamed up with their breath as he talked. She listened, teeth still chattering, not saying a word.

He told her about the emergency in Moosonee and the sick pilot, his awful Christmas at his sister-in-law's, that he'd missed practically the entire hunting season. Then he said that he'd missed *her*.

When he stopped, she said, "Oh."

She looked sheepish now. Said that it felt so good to be thawing out. Unzipping her red jacket, she exhaled, her eyes properly on his for the first time.

"I'm sorry," she said in a small voice, smiling feebly. Then she flicked her tongue along her bottom lip. Very slowly. And something about the way she did it made him interpret it as an invitation.

So he moved nearer to her on the bench seat, sliding his bum over a claw hammer and an empty cookie bag. He put his arm along the back of the bench and pulled her to him. Their mouths met. And it was a long kiss, hard and sustained, tongues exploring, arms and hands finding their way around each other's necks in their eagerness to reconnect. It was sweet, too. So sweet. He tasted the chocolate bar she'd eaten. Felt his body grow hot, oppressed by his thick parka.

With his mouth still glued to hers, he slid his hand under her jacket and encountered what felt like a wool sweater. He pushed it up. Fumbled for the top of her pants. Thrust his hand in, down between her legs, feeling warmth and wetness down there. He pulled the hand out again and leaned back, his eyes not moving from hers. He smelled the ends of his fingers. Licked them. Pushed two of them into her mouth.

She closed her lips around the fingers, sucking slowly, deliberately, flicking their length gently with her tongue as she moved her mouth up and down, up and down. When she stopped, he pushed his face under her messy hair and nibbled her neck, her nose, one of her ears. The ear felt very cold, oddly like a cube of refrigerated cheese he'd eaten on the flight back to Toronto from Moosonee.

Yet how aroused he felt with his lips on that ear, filled with longing, wanting to have the rest of her, yet at the same time not wanting to, because this teenage petting at the side of a snowy road in the middle of nowhere excited him in the way it had at the cabin. It was like nothing he'd experienced in years. Her smell on his fingers. The smooching. The sucking, The squirming on the seat of his pick up as their bodies sought each other.

* * *

The whole lusty story is available as a paperback or e-book from Amazon.com and in some independent bookstores. www.soniaday.com

GARLIC

Garlic increases blood flow
And that is what is needed
To make him stand up straight and tall
So play is unimpeded.

So cook a dish chock full of it
And keep a breath mint handy.
Share the dish and hopefully
You'll both be delightfully randy!

Icy Hot
A. Mack Lauren

He licked the windowpanes and drummed on the side of the old house.

"It's all right," I said rubbing my dog's ear. He whined again. "He'll be home soon."

Fire crackled in the wood stove. It was warm inside but the storm worried me. Liam worried me. He'd been away on business overseas and should have been back yesterday. I'd been ready for him yesterday. My panties had been damp from the excitement of his return yesterday. It was a delicious pressure I'd let build in his absence.

But the flame was doused when I'd gotten the call. His flight was delayed a day by the storm, grounded somewhere on the East Coast.

I moved to stand by the window. Pictures of our two children and our new tiny grandson smiled at me from the walls. Being a grandmother was an interesting experience. At 55 I was still young and strong enough to keep up with him but happy to say goodbye at the end of the visit. Being empty-nesters suited Liam and I better than I could've ever hoped.

"Mmm," I groaned.

Shit. I could feel the sweet dampness building between my legs. I was wet again. Liam needed to get home. He'd been gone too long this time.

I frowned at the sleet-covered forest that surrounded our property. It was getting worse.

I traced a slow line through the condensation on the window with my fingers while my other hand gently brushed my breast through the fabric of my button-down top. I squeezed my eyes tight and gasped in surprise at the taunt buds my nipples instantly became.

The fire popped against the wood stove's glass door. The wind clapped against the house. The power flickered once, twice and the lights went out. Hot red fire was the only light left in the room.

The dog whined and went to hide upstairs.

"Damn it Liam," I spat. I wanted him home. My body needed him home.

But I knew him. As a fit 56 year old, he had a lot of time left with his company. He didn't want to retire. Sometimes he had to be away.

I ran my frustrated fingers through my hair. It was short now. Liam used to like it long, but as he'd aged he changed. Grew up.

God, I thought as I moved to sit by the stove, *how he'd changed.*

I grinned into the fire and remembered Liam's seventeen-year-old body. Lean and strong. Liam's farm was one concession from my parents' so I'd met him in elementary school but didn't really *know* him until I'd hit a growth spurt and grew breasts in high school.

I'd been sweaty from a day's work moving hay-bales in

the barn when he rode up through the field on his dark horse.

"Hey Sharon," he said sitting tall above me in his saddle. His brown hair was messy from the ride and hung in thick waves over his forehead and ears. His hooded eyes shamelessly raked over me and he grinned.

I'd forgotten I unbuttoned my top scandalously low, attempting relief from the heat of the work in the barn. He could see my bra and the droplets of sweat clinging to my chest and stomach straight down my shirt. I flushed, embarrassed and started to turn away to right myself.

"Don't," he said reaching for me.

I eyed him suspiciously.

"Leave it." His voice was husky and raw.

He looked over his shoulder toward my parents' house, whatever message or errand forgotten, and offered me his hand.

"Come on Sharon."

I blushed again but let him pull me up in front of him on the saddle. His rigid manhood pressed into my back as his legs tightened around me to control the horse.

I gasped.

His lips brushed my ear. "Like that?" he asked.

I'd leaned into him and held the saddle horn for all it was worth. "Yes," I whispered.

I was nervous and trembling. I didn't know what was happening; why the hard head of the horn moving against my most private places was making me pant.

With one hand on the reins, he gently ran the other up the inside of my thigh. "Good."

He kicked the horse and our bodies moved in rhythm with

each other until we were lost in the forest between out parents' properties.

When we stopped he kissed me. His tongue touched mine, meeting little resistance as he opened my shirt. His rough farmer's hands were gentle on my newly budding mounds. And on the forest floor, he took my virginity as gently as any lusting teenage boy could.

I shivered remembering that first time.

The sharp bell of the phone pulled me from my memory.

I jumped to answer it, "Liam?"

"Miss me Sharon?" There was laughter in his voice.

I flushed. "Where are you?"

He chuckled deeply, sending a teasing shiver through me, "I'm on my way baby. The roads are—"

He cut out.

"Liam? How long until you get here?" I yelled into the phone.

I heard his laugher again, broken in the reception this time.

"Liam, this is not funny. I'm hor—worried about you," I caught myself.

"Keep the home fires burning honey. I'm at— "

The phone line went dead.

I growled as I slammed the phone into it's cradle.

Outside the trees were bending and cracking under the weight of the ice. It wasn't fair I was so hot when the world was frozen around me.

I threw some wood onto the fire brushed the dirt from my curving hips and thighs. They were considerably wider then when I fell in love with Liam but he didn't care. After baring two of his children the curve of my body was evidence of his claim on me. I was his.

I took my chair by the fire and began slowly, gently rocking my pelvis against its edge. Built up pressure spread, warmth reaching down to my toes. I began to pant. I wasn't sure I could wait for him. Oh, but I wanted too. I wanted Liam.

I caught my breath and focused on the fingers of the flames caressing each other, moving into one another against the pane of glass then separating again.

I started thinking how Liam and I had lost touch in college. Spread apart like the moving flames. Liam usually had a different girl from his business school on his arm when our lives crossed paths but we remained friends. I dated some nice men in college. I had good sex.

But no matter how many men touched my body I couldn't fade the memory of the wild, spontaneous, unschooled lovemaking I'd had with Liam. There was something else I couldn't ignore; how he looked at me on those scarce meetings we had. No matter how long it'd been, he'd rake his eyes over me possessively, hungrily. No matter who I was with, it would make me flush, my body react. And he knew it. But when we had experimented with dating others, he didn't touch me.

Not until after we finished college. His family had a Christmas party at their farm. I was recently single and it was one of the few parties I'd seen him at without a woman. He'd changed, now 30, his hair was still dark and styled longer than most, but neat, for business. He'd lost his tan but his jaw was square and his eyes were dark. He'd become hardened, guarded even. I knew something, or someone had done that to him.

I caught him staring at me with sensual, hooded eyes more than once that evening.

I'd changed too. No longer the inexperienced girl I'd been when we were together in high school, the premature gray I covered with highlights a testament to it, I knew what he wanted. And what I wanted.

We'd been left alone in his parents' living room for the briefest moment; Liam sat on the couch across from me clearly tormented, trying to tell me something. I'd had enough of his haunted silence and met his eyes with coy, teasing half smile and lifted my skirt. Slightly. Like I was adjusting it.

It rode up my thigh and I uncrossed my legs giving him a full naked view of my bikini-waxed triangle of dark curls. His eyes widened. The fabric of his pants became tight around his growing erection.

"Sharon," he growled my name like a warning.

His uncle stepped in to join us with wine. I crossed my legs discretely, accepted the drink and carried on like nothing had happened.

At dinner Liam sat across from me.

He stared at me then raised his eyebrow in challenge before he ran his foot up my inner thigh under the table. My fork clattered on my plate. He grinned as I apologized to his mother for my table manners.

I hardly ate a thing.

All through dinner he stroked me until my breathing was all I could focus on. Trying to breath normally so our families wouldn't notice me on the edge of climaxing at the table. He didn't stop when my breath caught and became hoarse or my mother asked if I was all right when I squirmed in my seat, pressing my self against him. And, oh God, I didn't want him to stop.

"Like that?" he asked.

I gasped and stared at him. Our families turned to us.

Then I looked at the pie someone had put on my plate and flushed. "Yes," I practically moaned. We both knew I wasn't talking about dessert.

He gave the barest hint of a nod toward the front door. "Leave it," he said softly. "My parents still keep horses. I'll show you." He rounded the table and held out his hand for me. "Come on Sharon."

I could remember Liam following me out to the barn. His shoulder bumping mine. His breath ragged.

I stepped into the stable. It was warm and clean. The horses shuffled softly in their stalls. He gently closed the door behind him, turned and caught my wrist, pulling me too him.

My hips pressed into his throbbing erection, rigid and large against my leg. One hand held me firmly to his body the other flexed at the nape of my neck.

"It's been too long," he groaned. His lips left a trail of hot kisses from the soft skin behind my ear down my throat.

I'd curled my fingers into his jacket at his chest. "Too long since you've had sex?" I'd asked lightly.

He caught my lips and leaned his forehead against mine. I tilted my face toward his and watched as he squeezed his hard, guarded eyes shut. He'd exhaled. "Too long, since I've had sex with you, Sharon."

Then my Jacket was off, my skirt pushed up over my hips. His hands cupped my buttocks as I fumbled to pull his jacket over his shoulders. When I managed, his dress shirt came with it. Buttons rattled to the floor.

My fingers ran through his chest hair, brushed over solid muscles and gripped his shoulders. He lifted me against him, and my legs wrapped around his waist.

All the gentle patience he'd held in check inside evaporated. His lips crushed mine. His tongue parted my lips and explored as freely as his hands on my ass. He ran his fingers along the inside of my thigh then penetrated.

My moan was swallowed in our kiss. Sweet pleasure only Liam and I had together erupted. He turned and pressed my back into the wall and his teasing, prodding fingers deepened. I gasped for air against his lips. My head tilted back.

"Come for me, Sharon," he coaxed, watching as my lips part.

I felt the unstoppable flood of hot tremors release delicious pressure and I came against his fingers.

"Beautiful," he whispered as I collapsed onto his chest. I breathed in his intoxicating scent. His hands moved to my waist then slowly slid up under my shirt. He stopped just under my breasts. I clung to him. My hands wrapped around his neck and tangled in his hair. He met my eyes. His were still so dark.

"Touch me, Liam," I said. His fingers flexed against my skin. "Please," I begged then pulled his mouth to mine and scraped his bottom lip with my teeth. His thumbs flicked over my nipples, and I arched with a sharp cry of surprise. My shirt was over my head. He squeezed my breast through the fabric of my black lace bra.

"You're beautiful," he said and pulled my breasts free so they hung over the delicate fabric. He took one in his mouth and bit gently, then with more urgency, harder.

My nails dug into his shoulders and I cried out, so wet the inside of my thighs were damp.

"I want you," I panted.

He laughed against my breast flicking the nipple with his tongue and entwined my fingers in his, pulling them from behind his neck.

Releasing my breast he met my eyes and brushed his lips to mine, "Say it again Sharon." He closed his eyes, closing off whatever hurt was hiding there while pulling my hands down the length of his body to rest on his hips. "Say it," he rasped.

My pulse was jumping, my breath uneven, my back arched with desire, my womanhood wet and throbbing. I opened his pants and reached inside. He sucked in his breath and opened his eyes, trying to read me.

"Liam, how could you not know I want you? I want you now," I whispered. "Fuck me."

He exhaled with relief and desire then tipped his head back and groaned deep and hot while I stroked him.

"Sharon, I've wanted this for so long. I've wanted you so bad."

His pants hit the floor. He grunted as he lifted one of my legs. My ass pressed into the wall. "I had to watch you come and go with those other men. Knowing they were fucking you." His mouth crushed mine again and he thrust into me with all the impatience and grace he had when we where seventeen.

I was full, stretched to my limit and cried out. His tongue drowned it out. He began to move, slowly, still holding my leg off the floor. He grunted with the effort of his restraint.

"Come on, Liam," I panted and bent to press my tongue across his flat nipple.

"Oh Fuck Sharon!" His control shattered, he pounded me against the wall with hard thrusts that sent pleasure exploding through clenching muscles, tightening around him in my body. My scream of pleasure mixed with his triumphant moan. He shuddered, arched his back, driving deeper into me, and calling out in release.

He dropped my leg and crushed my body as he collapsed into me, pinning me between him and the wall while he struggled to catch his breath. His seed ran a warm trail down my leg.

He took a deep breath and touched his sheen covered forehead to mine. His fists clenched the rumpled fabric of my skirt still pushed up around my waist.

"I think I should marry you, Sharon," he said. His breath quickened, his eyes guarded, narrow . . . and serious.

I tilted my head, brushed my lips softly across his and smiled.

Our oldest son was conceived that night. I smiled now at the memory and pressed my pelvis against the edge of the chair, teasing, stoking the fire that burned in me. It wasn't enough. I wanted Liam inside me.

My hands thumbed over my breasts. I unfastened the buttons of my shirt and squeezed the naked flesh, hard. God, I wanted his hands on me. My head dropped back as my nipples stood erect. I pinched them delicately as I continued to rock.

When my fingers found their way to the wet heat burning between my legs I knew I couldn't wait. The sweet nub of flesh was plumb and throbbing. I began to stroke.

The fire crackled. Ice pelted the side of the house and my sharp cries became higher and more panted as I continued to pleasure myself. The sense of urgency building, threatening to explode, on the edge of the delicious release I wanted so desperately.

I pulled my fingers back. They were wet with my desire and I shuddered against my compounding need for organism and clamped two of my slick members together. Gently I pressed them between the soft, dripping lips of my longing and called out in a frustrated groan as they entered my tight, trembling body.

I moved my fingers in and out, in and out. Slowly first, but as I quickly neared the edge of organism again my fingers began to pulse with the rhythm of my staggered gasps. I clamped my nipple between my fingers and pulled, hard.

The swell of excitement pushed me to the edge. There was no stopping the heat that threaten to burn me alive. My legs open wide in anticipation. Thrusting and grunting against my fingers, taking them all they way, I wished they were deeper, I wished it was Liam inside me.

God Liam. My head tilted, eyes rolling back. The ice and fire muffled my scream as my whole body convulsed. My fingers were crushed in the waves of unstoppable pulses within my body. I sat ridged, eyelids fluttering as I lapped up every tremor, wishing I could lap up Liam's spent seed as well.

I leaned back in the chair trying to catch my breath, slow my racing pulse. My fingers slipped from my body and I traced wet rings around my nipples before collapsing into tormented sleep.

The draft on my naked skin woke me before the soft click of the door latch.

"Hey Sharon," Liam smiled knowingly down at me.

"Liam!"

His brown hair was messy from his long trip home and clung in damp waves over his forehead from the storm. His hooded eyes raked over me shamelessly, possessively, hot with need.

I'd forgotten my shirt and pants were open. He could see my breast hanging loose traced with the dried evidence of my orgasm. I flushed, embarrassed I couldn't wait for him and started to right myself.

"Don't," he said reaching for me. "Leave it."

I eyed him passionately as he bent and cupped my breast. His mouth met mine roughly then covered my already rock hard nipple.

I arched, gasping with delight.

His lips brushed my other breast in turn. "Like that?" he said against my heaving flesh.

My fingers hastily worked to unfasten his pants. "Yes," I breathed.

He grabbed my shirt and snapped it over my shoulders as he pulled me out of the chair, pressing me to kneel before him.

"Good," he growled, the darkness long disappeared from his eyes. They were no longer haunted but strong, confident.

His pants were gone and his manhood throbbed large and unyielding. His eyes and the set of his jaw were taunt with his fiery lust.

Deliberately, slowly, he wrapped his fingers around the nape of my neck and guided me to him. "Show me how much you missed me baby," he teased.

I looked into his eyes. He flexed his fingers and I trembled. God, he could still make me tremble.

He grinned, knowing the power he had over me.

"Come on Sharon," he commanded.

The fire inside cast hot, orange shadows over our bodies as I licked my lips in anticipation and the storm outside beat its icy fingers over the house.

"In all your Amours you should prefer old Women to young ones."

Benjamin Franklin

Indigo Night
Judy Zarowny

Our bodies expanding
glistening with raindrops
moon dust and fireflies
sparkle and dance
Murmuring, shuddering
riding a comet of
shimmering starlight
blessed in the warmth
of an indigo trance.

Moon drenched and glistening
fragrant and shivering
ribbons of fireflies
dance between lips
pulsing and thrusting
expanding contracting
expanding
contracting.
In rhythm like flight
blessed in the glow
of an indigo night.

The Green Man
Marjorie Gold

It was after menopause that she first started dreaming about the green man. The first time it happened she awoke in the middle of the night, drenched. At first she thought it was night sweats, but they had faded away years ago. No, this was different. Her heart was pounding and she was wet between her legs.

It had been years since she and her husband made love. In fact, she was afraid that intercourse was no longer possible. So much had dried up in her life—romance, passion, intimacy. Was it a surprise that her own inner juice seemed to be gone, too?

To be quite honest, sex had never been that high on her priority list. As a young woman, in her twenties and thirties, she enjoyed it, most of the time, but that, of course, often depended on her partner. She was not a free spirit, not really, not in bed. There were only a few men, when she looked back at her life, who touched her, literally and metaphorically, in ways she would never forget.

There was Timothy, the ruggedly handsome actor who she fell wildly in love with, but who fell wildly in love with someone else. There was Rick, the one-night cowboy with the red snakeskin boots. But maybe that was exciting because she never saw him again. And there was Chester, the man almost twenty years her senior, the boxer and poet, with the crumpled nose and tender hands, who made love to her when she was eighteen, in ways that no man before or after ever did. She had dreams of running away with him, like all the storybooks promised, but she quickly discovered that life was not always full of happy endings.

Yet, she weathered those storms. She grew up to be a decent woman, a good wife, and a good mother. Her husband was a kind and caring man. All of her friends told her so—many admitted their own jealousy. "You don't know how lucky you are."

She knew she was lucky. She owned a lovely home and a new car, thanks to her husband's hard work, and she was in good health, and had a bright, sweet son. Of course, motherhood had not been easy for her. She gave birth at 45 years old, unusually late, and even though everything went very well, she slid silently into postpartum depression. But her husband stood by her side and after two years of therapy and anti-depressants, the dark cloud lifted. She had everything, really. If there was a necklace or a dress she liked, her husband told her to buy it. If she wanted to go away for the weekend to visit a girlfriend, her husband said, go ahead, we'll be fine.

So it was with all this goodness and comfort that she entered the third phase of her womanhood—menopause—and emerged, a little heavier, a little more wrinkled, but without too many scars.

Except for the dreams about the green man.

In the first dream he appeared only briefly. She was walking in a forest, not unlike the woods behind her home. Except these were bigger and darker and seemed to go on for a long, long time. She somehow knew she was far from her house, far from her neighborhood. It was twilight. And she didn't understand, when she thought about the dream later, trying to analyze it, why she was walking deeper into the woods. That's not like me, she told herself. I would never go deeper in the woods, certainly not at twilight.

But dream selves are brave. So she walked into the shadows, calmly, comfortably, as if she knew exactly where she was heading. And as she did, she felt him. At first it was just a tingling in the back of her neck. But soon the sensation grew, trickling down her spine, tingling within her chest, moving down her legs. It was as if her whole body was a tuning fork—and she was resonating *to him*.

Suddenly she heard a branch snap. She stopped, looked slowly around, and thought she saw him. A man's outline, between two trees, tall and broad. But it didn't last—and she questioned seeing it. As she took another step, she heard a loud rustling. This time she froze, her heart beating faster, the tingling sensation filling her body.

A wisp of wind teased past her hair. She closed her eyes with pleasure. That's when she heard it. Barely a whisper.

Come to me.

Then she awoke.

The second time she dreamed about him was a week later. She and her husband had fought over something trivial. She was trying to cook healthier food and switched from white rice to brown. Neither her son nor husband liked the chewier grain. Both rebelled and refused to eat it. It made her angry—and she told him later, "If you don't eat it, then he won't."

"Why should he?" her husband asked. "It didn't taste great."

A small argument, but she couldn't let go of it. She pushed.

"Brown rice is better for you," she said. "All the experts say so. We have to learn to like it."

"Why?" he asked again. "What's the big deal? Let's just stick with white rice."

"No!" she burst out, and suddenly tears flowed down her cheeks. "No! I want us to eat brown rice. And you have to set an example!" She threw down the striped cotton dish towel and stormed upstairs.

Later, after she apologized and they watched their favorite TV show, she kissed him goodnight and excused herself. "I'm tired," she said, and went up to bed.

She washed her face, brushed and flossed her teeth, as she always did, put on her cotton pajamas, and climbed into bed. *Why did I make such a big deal about brown rice*, she wondered. But she drifted off to sleep before she could find the answer.

This time she was standing in a shopping mall. But this mall had no walls or ceilings. It was in the middle of dark woods and the only stores were food stores and gourmet kitchen stores like most upscale malls have. But the only thing they sold were bowls of brown and white rice. Big bowls, small bowls— ceramic, glass, plastic—all filled with hard white grains or hard brown ones.

Yet she walked past the empty stores, uninterested. She was alone in this dream mall—but what held her attention was the vast night sky. She could see stars everywhere. *They look like tiny grains of shimmering rice,* she thought. *Maybe the whole world is really made of rice.*

At the end of the corridor, there was a door with a small black sign: No Admittance. She knew instantly that she had to go through.

How strange, she thought later, after she awoke, trying again to analyze the dream. I would never go through that door in real life.

But she did. And there he was.

At first she didn't see him because she was standing in darkness, with only starlight to illuminate her path. But as soon as her eyes adjusted she saw a man, a few yards away. And instantly she knew it was him

Come to me, he said.

He was tall with wild dark hair. She could only see his outline. Broad shoulders, long legs. As she took a step toward him, she noticed, with a soft gasp, that he was not wearing any clothes. At least that's what it looked like. As she approached him, he came clearer into view. His skin was a dark greenish brown; his hair the same color, in curls, wild and windblown. His arms and chest were covered with matted leaves and twigs, as if he had fallen onto wet ground in the forest. Wrapped around his waist were broad green leaves, covering him the way a tribal man might dress, at least in her imagination.

When she was a few feet away, she stopped. Her heart pounded in her chest. He held her gaze for a long time.

"Would you do something for me?" he asked. His voice was deep and soft and honest.

Without hesitating, she nodded.

"Close your eyes."

She did as he asked. She stood there, listening to her own breathing. Everything was still. She could hear the night birds. She could feel the cool darkness on her skin. Then, suddenly, he was behind her, his warm breath, his lips brushing her neck. She swallowed hard, barely able to contain herself.

"Don't move," he said.

She wanted to cry out. She felt wildly guilty and excited. Her breathing quickened.

"Let go," he whispered into her ear. His hands moved slowly, carefully, over her body.

For an instant, she opened her eyes. The glittering rice stars took hold of her.

"Let go," he repeated softly.

And she did.

In the morning she lay in bed for a long time. She told her husband she didn't feel well. He kissed her on the forehead and said he would get their son ready for school. It was only after they left the house that she finally got up. In the bathroom, she looked into the mirror the way she always did every morning of her life. The face that looked back was clearly not young any more. Soft brown eyes, sagging cheeks, a wrinkled neck. Yet today, instead of turning away in despair like she usually did, she looked deeper. The brown eyes that gazed back seemed brighter this morning.

She reached up, and for the first time in years, tenderly touched her face. The skin was soft and smooth, the complexion clear. I'm really not so unattractive, she thought. Slowly, she ran her fingers through her gray brown hair, closing her eyes momentarily, enjoying the sensation. Then she splashed ice cold water on her face.

Maybe today I'll cook a new dish, she thought. Something I've never made before. As she brushed her teeth vigorously, the answer came. Rice pudding, she thought, with a smile. And she headed downstairs to meet the day.

"Edwina always enjoyed a morning ride. Some mornings she rode the horse, and some mornings she rode the groom."

Barbara Taylor Bradford

ICE CREAM

Ice Cream might be chilly
Or even downright cold
Putting it on warm skin therefore
Is being mighty bold!

The shock will stir the senses,
And maybe raise a yelp
But as it melts and dribbles down
They'll need a little help.

So use your tongue to chase it
And see where it will go.
That little river winding down
And you must stop the flow.

Or let it run until it gets
To your very favourite spot
You'll both be very happy
When you find what you have sought.

The flavour doesn't matter,
Let gravity do its work.
Prepare yourself to have some fun,
But please try not to smirk.

Mrs. W

Eve Milan

5 a.m.

Felina is the girl next door. She is Mrs. W's nocturnal neighbor. Felina is the insufferable one who laughs easily because nothing is more important than this moment.

Mrs. W did not laugh easily. It hadn't always been this way but when her husband passed away nine years ago, somehow he had taken her smile with him. Perhaps that is what made it insufferable to hear the sound of laughter outside her apartment.

Thump! Like a body banging against her front door. Then another *Thump!*

The first noise startled her. The second *whump!* could have made her mad but instead, it acted like a curiosity magnet and she was drawn to have a peek.

It was not all that unusual for her neighbor to use the hallway as a launching pad for lovemaking and anyone who did this surely wanted to be watched.

In her pink fluffy slippers Mrs. W. crept up to the door. Although *they* were doing nothing to keep the noise level down, somehow it felt like the decent thing to approach with respectful silence. Just as she approached, Felina pushed her man up against the wall across the hall directly opposite her door.

Mrs. W caught a glimpse of his handsome face, covered in dark stubble, before Felina's kiss covered it from her view.

Mrs. W couldn't remember the last time she had laughed out loud, and hearing Felina's flowing giggles irritated her . . . yet, like a moth drawn to a flame, she found herself gravitating toward the sound. Felina had often said that having fun was a basic human right. She expected it. And she got it.

With her cheek pressed against her front door, Mrs. W in apartment 507 had an excellent view of the hallway outside apartment 508. More precisely, of Felina.

Felina. The tart next door.

Four feet of corridor stood between their two apartments and their totally opposing lives.

Felina's silver rhinestone stilettos drew the eyes upward past perfect legs. Her midnight blue, short leather skirt seemed to deliberately show the tops of her garters. Black clasps gripped fishnet stockings, exposing a gaping rip no doubt made from feverish fingers.

Mrs. W wondered if it was he who had made the hole. She turned away from the view of another world seen through a dime-sized window. Her hand fussed with the small hole in the left side pocket of her robe. How long had that been there?

It was nothing like the hole in Mrs. W's life. Her late husband had been her one and only love, and in spite of well-intentions of Mrs. B, a friend from church, who incessantly wanted to fix her up with one of her seven balding cousins, Mrs. W wasn't ready to date. "You still look pretty good," Mrs. B had said, looking her over. "But we all have an expiration date."

Those conversations with Mrs. B always made her feel worse. It wasn't that she was unhappy. It was just that somehow she felt the glass of her life was half empty and she didn't know how to fill it.

Mrs. W couldn't remember when she'd lost her smile. It used to be part of her everyday life, something she took for granted. Where do you look for something like that?

Perhaps through a peephole. Perhaps you borrow a glimpse of someone else's happiness. Mrs. W turned her sights back to her window on that other world.

Felina grabbed the back of his curly hair, and pulled her lips away from his, to catch a breath. She turned and looked right at the peephole. He turned to see what was more compelling than his lips.

Mrs. W froze. Did they know she was watching them?

She backed her eye away, held her breath, careful not to make a sound or move a shadow that would reveal her presence from the half inch gap under the edge of the door. She wished she had remembered to turn out her light. Too late now.

Without the peephole view—her window on the exotic world across the hall—she could only listen now. The tiny nerve endings in her ear woke up fully to the task of feeding her imagination.

She heard the jangle of the bracelets that snaked halfway up Felina's arm. What was she doing with that hand? Where was it moving? Did it like what it was feeling?

Was it safe to look again?

Her hungry eye drew her back to the hole. The fox hole. The whole forbidden fruit on the other side of her door.

With one bold eye she watched as his black cowboy boot pushed Felina's legs apart. Mrs. W could smell his musky desire. Or was she imagining that?

His leg thrust between Felina's, and her head banged against the wall. But her face said it didn't hurt. Said it was naughty. Naughty and ever so nice.

Mrs. W felt the urge to interrupt them. Stop all that fun. This is not what hallways are for.

But she made no move to stop them. She had to see how far they would go.

Mrs. W knew it wasn't polite to watch. She was not a rude person but this minor crime seemed to be negated by the major act of those who would put on such a scintillating show in a public corridor.

Mrs. W heard the chimes of her grandfather clock. 5 AM. The Sunday newspaper would be waiting at her door. The perfect excuse for her accidental corridor appearance. She must have her Sunday paper, with all the ads for the best prices on produce. Sometimes if she didn't get the paper early, some amoral neighbor would abscond with it. Her fingers trembled as she unfastened the chain lock, turned the tumbler, and unbolted the bottom lock.

One quarter turn of the doorknob and her world opened into theirs.

He looked at Mrs. W with smoldery up-all-night eyes. Slow motion muscles moved in a black leather rebel jacket, as he turned to look at her. His heavy breath made his chest—in his tight black shirt—rise and fall. An antique silver cross clung to his neck. She wondered if it had been his mother's. Been awhile since he'd shaved.

Mrs. W shivered in her faded flannel robe. His penetrating slow sucking-in-every-inch gaze made her feel naked.

"Sorry, Mrs. W," Felina's sultry telephone-sex voice purred. "Were we being too loud?"

Mrs. W was too trapped by his gaze to answer.

"This is José," Felina offered.

José said nothing.

José let his fingers do the talking.

With his eyes on Mrs. W, José slid his middle finger inside Felina.

Her whimper of pleasure didn't distract him from his mission. How did he know Mrs. W couldn't look away? His hand slowly slid up and down, mesmerizing two for one.

She could see he liked the feeling of power. Using one woman to affect another. His one motion linking their sensations.

Felina's quivers let Mrs. W know how well he knew what he was doing.

The thick Sunday morning paper lay on the floor between them, nearer to them than her. She could grab it, and her hand would be closer to his raked cowboy heel. But she couldn't move.

"You want it?" His voice had that too-many-hard-nights harshness. Was he talking about the newspaper—or something else? She froze. Bambi in his headlights. Fear, and her pink fuzzy slippers, glued her to the spot.

Without leaving Felina's inner realm, he reached down, hoisted the heavy paper with his other hand, and held it out to Mrs. W.

Even though shrouded in her robe, she felt his male instincts scan her female curves. It seemed he could tell she still had them in all the right places. His eyes moved to the sash as if to say, one tug would open her robe. This thought made her grasp her sash. A mixed-message? A quiet invitation?

Yes, she wanted it. It was why she had opened her door.

She reached for the paper.

"I need to see where apples are on sale." her first idiotic words. Nothing else to do except spew some more. "I was planning to bake a pie and …"

"I like pie," he said.

The way he said it, suddenly made the simple words lose their clear meaning.

She could smell Felina's response to his sliding hand. Could even see her glistening wetness on his fingers when they slid downwards.

All the time José held Mrs. W in his eyes.

Primal flight, fight and freeze impulses flooded her brain, rendering her instantly helpless under his controlling upper hand.

Desperate to regain control of her own body's impulses, she backed away. Somehow, she managed to close Pandora's door.

Best to put a distance between them. Safe from the feelings he ignited, she tried to catch her breath. Yes, she was back on the inside, trying hard to quiet her mind, to erase the memory. To vanquish the scent of them from her memory.

She was back in her quiet world.

He was outside. Where it was steamy and unpredictable.

But he was still—ever so —just outside her door.

Her sense-memory of him held him right there. A phantom with enough power to reach through the door.

And touch her.

No. Lock the door.

No, don't.

Yes. Lock it loudly so he'll know you don't want . . .

Her fingers trembled on the locks. Just as they had when she had opened them.

Safe is better. Better to dream about a perfectly remembered José. The real one is far too dangerous.

The real one is far too close. Far too real.

She walked toward her kitchen. There must be something there to do. But a moment later she found herself returning to the front door. As she listened to Felina's rising moan, her heart beat faster.

Sunday Afternoon

Mrs. W sat in her kitchen, mending the hole in her pink fluffy robe. The pies she had made earlier were cooling nicely.

She had made two.

The irritating click of the kitchen clock reminded her it was only ten after one and she had already finished all the tasks on her To Do list. She hadn't been able to go back to sleep after. After seeing. After hearing. After everything about José.

A shiny gold key on a Playboy bunny chain sat on the shelf, looking garishly out of place between her collection of Queen Anne Tea Cups.

Keys can be taunting. Especially when they could open Felina's front door. It was a cruel irony that Mrs. W held the tantalizing key to the Temptress in 508.

One night she had even considered putting the bunny keys in an envelope with Felina's return address and slipping them to Robbie. Robbie was the bagger in Safeway with the bangs falling in his eyes. The trophy at the end of the aisle she always chose because he always had an easy smile. But she didn't smile back. Not because she didn't want to smile. It was just that she had lost her way to the easy smile.

Although Robbie and Mrs. W had only exchanged a few words, she had watched him moving through the aisles, stopping to help the pretty young girls find something they could easily find themselves. She knew enough about Robbie to know he would use the mystery key. So the next time she accepted his sweet invitation to carry her bags to her car, walking next to her with his shy-new-boy-toy scent, she would hand him Felina's keys. She had more than once imagined what might have happened if he used them. If he came to her door and be used by Felina.

Maybe she should use the key. Right now.

Sneak over and see if José was the kind of guy that let Felina sleep all tangled up around him.

No. Don't do that.

Besides, he was probably the kind that slept solo even when there was a woman in the same bed. Just inches away he would remain a stranger on a remote-island-pillow. He was definitely a sleeping-on-the-edge kind of guy. Probably born with the sixth sense for the vaginal exit sign.

Or maybe they weren't sleeping. Maybe his lips were on hers. Doing it again. With their morning's urgency.

Mrs. W promised herself that today she would make Felina take back her key. It was too much of a mental burden. She never did buy Felina's version of the motive for her possession of a mode of entry to apartment 508. "In case of emergency," the envelope taped to her door explained. "To feed the goldfish."

It was true that Felina was utterly devoted to Goldie, Gilda and Bruce. She had three because, as she explained, "Even goldfish like to have a ménage now and then."

The real reason Mrs. W was in possession of the key to The Den of Goldfish Iniquity was because since she had moved in six months ago Felina had already lost her keys four times. Somehow Felina had sufficient foresight to order the gold bunny key chains online at the discount rate for procuring a dozen at a time, yet she consistently made the tactical error of never discovering they were MIA—Missing in Action—before 3 AM. Each inebriated de-bunnied incident came with another apologetic knock on Mrs. W's door, another convoluted story and another handsome man in tow.

In her whole life Mrs. W had never lost *her* keys.

Then she heard a strong knock which startled her from the musing of an imaginary mission of research and intelligence gathering in Felina's apartment 508. No one ever knocked. Except Felina.

Ignoring her knock provided a feeling of power. But this minor thrill of victory did not make the knocking stop. Probably because Felina and the word "no" were not on speaking terms this year.

Felina had once told Mrs. W that every New Year's Eve

she resolved to eliminate a word from her vocabulary for 365 days. She would cease and desist to indulge a word that "desaturated life experience."

This year she had eliminated the word "no."

Felina described the loss of those two sequential letters as "an awesome act of liberation."

"Mrs. *Double-youuuuuu* It's me, Felina."

Mrs. W pretended she wasn't home. Which did not fool Felina.

"I need to borrow some cream and sugar," she said in her *you're the only one in the whole world who can save me* voice.

Mrs. W told herself she would ignore this plea. And any future pleas.

Told herself this as she walked over to open the door.

To tell her that. To tell her this was the last time—

Felina was leaning against her door, holding her empty Snow White coffee mug. She looked like a cross between a train wreck and a glowing goddess, depending upon which angle she revealed.

Without waiting for an invitation, she floated past her. Sliding inside. Penetrating Mrs. W's orderly world.

She wore *his* black T shirt.

Only.

It wasn't very long on him either. It carried his scent as she moved past Mrs. W to the kitchen.

Mrs. W left her door ajar, on the assumption that this was going to be a brief encounter once she put her foot down.

"I swear to God, I am giving up Tequila," Felina announced, helping herself to a cup of coffee. Mrs. W always made a full pot.

Felina grabbed the cow cream pitcher and poured an excessive amount of cream. "I so need this," Felina said.

Did she mean the coffee?

Ignoring the fact that Mrs. W had not invited her to sit, she plopped herself down and took a deep inhalation of the French Roast inhalation.

"Aroma is the foreplay to the taste. Don't you think?" Felina asked.

Mrs. W didn't answer.

"Sit down," Felina said as if this was *her* kitchen table, her cream and her very own *Felina in Wonderland* tea party.

Mrs. W watched how comfortable she was. Comfortable making herself at home in her home—like the prodigal daughter returning from a fresh year at college with her fill-er-up-please mug. It was most irritating how comfortable she was, being nearly naked, and wrapped in his scent.

Mrs. W never felt that comfortable, even alone in her own bed.

How dare Felina feel so comfortable. Mrs. W felt she and Felina were still in the "we barely know each other, there's a quarter of a century difference in our ages, I'm not sure I even like you, and we live in totally different universes" stage of relationship.

Felina saw it differently. She had explained it to Mrs. W one missing-key night when she had come in late from the pouring rain. Felina was not the kind of girl who called the weather station because that was too much planning ahead, and she never took an umbrella because she could never remember where she left it. So, sitting that night on Mrs. W's cozy couch, all snuggly and wrapped in Mrs. W's royal blue terry cloth towel, Felina had expounded on her philosophy of human interconnectivity.

With her wispy, crooked smile she had said, "All relationships have no beginning and no end, because if you're living in The Now, there is no past and no future."

Mrs. W had pondered those words many times. Sometimes finding great meaning and even a kind of soothing in them. Other times they felt like pancake batter that had been left out too long.

Sitting in her kitchen now, Felina had that same disarming smile. Felina smiled more times before lunch than Mrs. W did in a month.

"Sizzling," Felina said, which Mrs. W had learned meant "cool" but Felina said that word had been worn out. "You got brown sugar. I told you it was healthier."

Felina treated her Snow White coffee mug to a massive amount of brown sugar and slowly swirled her spoon in sweet anticipation.

Watching her inhale the fragrance, Mrs. W marveled at Felina's restraint.

"Delaying the pleasure until the very last moment makes the first virginal sip that much better," Felina said.

But apparently Felina's tank of self-restraint was suddenly empty. She took a loud, slurpy, satisfied sip and put her bare legs on the chair next to her.

Mrs. W's raised eyebrow made her take them down.

"Oh. Yeah, sorry. I know, legs on the table ain't lady-like."

Sorry? About legs on the table. After all she had revealed

the night before?

Mrs. W wondered if Felina's short term memory included the Hallway Peepshow in the wee hours. She really wanted to bring it up, but wasn't sure if it was appropriate coffee talk. She searched for the right deliberately vague words, and settled on, "Who was that young man?"

"What young man?"

"You said his name was José."

"Oh! José!" The memories poured over her. "I didn't think of him as a *young* man. He's so . . .so sublime."

Felina was now much more awake and alert, either from remembering José, or from the infusion of caffeine. She put down her Snow White mug. "Oh, wow, do I smell pies?"

Her eyes wandered to the counter and widened when she saw the pies. But Mrs. W couldn't let it go.

"I heard you two come home . . ."

"Two? Coming? Home?"

Mrs. W watched Felina scan her memory. Good. She doesn't remember. Mrs. W reveled in the power of holding a secret memory that Felina didn't have. But she couldn't help herself, and offered a memory jogging clue.

"In the hallway. He was . . ."

"Oh! The hallway," Felina blurted. "Wow! That man gives good hallway. I might be in love."

"So soon?"

"Well "love" in quotes. I'm in love with his—" Felina managed to curb her enthusiasm before she could say the word.

Mrs. W was ashamed to admit she wanted to hear the word.

Maybe even have a detail or two.

The clock ticked away, pecking at the silence between them. Felina sipped her coffee in morning after glory.

"Why did you make two pies?" she asked.

Mrs. W couldn't hold back any longer. "You're in love with his what?"

Felina smiled. "His cock."

She had no trouble using the word and sniffed her nose dangerously close to the pie that sat between them.

"What's so special about it?" Mrs. W asked, appalled at her need to know.

"It's smooth and—"

"And what?"

"And very suckable."

"Why? I mean what makes it . . . "

Felina jumped into Mrs. W's embarrassed puddle of silence.

"I like how it slides against me." She was happy to supply details. "And that it's not too thick."

Mrs. W wondered how thick 'not-too-thick' was.

Felina read her mind. She used her hands to define the circumference and length, to make the perfect picture come alive between them.

Mrs. W blushed with the sensation this image produced in her mind.

Felina saw this. One cup of Snow White made her miss nothing. "Want to see the shape of his head and everything?"

She didn't wait for an answer. She took the cow pitcher and ever so carefully poured a little puddle on the vinyl table cloth, and then caressed it into the shape of the member who wasn't there.

She scrutinized her creation like an artist and, seeking to capture perfection, made precise changes with her finger.

Then reasonably proud of the likeness, sat back to enjoy her recreation.

And there it was between them. Lying right there on her mauve vinyl table cloth. The white outline. Like at a crime scene.

Mrs. W couldn't take her eyes off it.

Maybe that's why they didn't hear him come in.

Looks just like me," José said, enjoying their liking his likeness.

He was wearing only a royal blue towel around his waist. Mrs. W couldn't help but notice it was the one missing from her set. Felina had a habit of borrowing without asking. He walked past them.

"Where are you going?" Felina asked, with a tone implying what ever was next was going to be fun.

"Shower" he replied.

Mrs. W's mouth dropped when she realized he meant hers.

José Enters . . . Her World

He was all fresh and wet from the shower and . . .still wrapped around his waist, hugging slim hips, was *her* royal blue towel.

Mrs. W couldn't even pretend to look anywhere else.

"Grab a cup," Felina offered. "In the cupboard over there."

José took instructions well. He chose the King of Hearts

souvenir mug Mrs. W had for more years than Felina had been breathing.

The Mystery of the Missing Royal Blue Towel from Mrs. W's set was clearly solved. She remembered loaning Felina the pink one last month when she had gotten caught in the downpour after the Gallery Opening after-party. After she had forgotten where she hid her keys at the after-after-party.

Mrs. W couldn't think about anything other than the fact that he was naked against her towel. Had he caught her sliding a peek? She forced her eyes upward. Since Felina had de-shirted him, his chest was delightfully bare.

This reincarnation of Michelangelo's model must have had his own key to Gold's Gym. Felina certainly had an eye for sculpture.

"Cream and sugar?" Felina offered, showing a domestic side of herself. One of the few sides of herself she hadn't exposed.

"Black." His voice dripped machismo.

Mrs. W caught it that Felina hadn't known him long enough to know how he liked his coffee. He poured his own cup with a careful, zen-like mindfulness, not spilling a drop, and wiping the bottom of the pot with a napkin before replacing it. She wondered who had taught him such manners.

Mrs. W was tempted to take a napkin and wipe away his likeness. Or would that be rude?

He took a seat between the two women and in the style of comfortable men, he didn't bother to close his legs. With just the act of sitting he had commanded the space, allowing his aura to penetrate the space between them.

The wall clock ticked. Or was it her heart making that racket? Mrs. W watched his eyes wander to the counter, taking in her sweet pies.

"You made two" he said, letting his eyes drink her blush.

"I thought you might . . .you know. Want it. Some. I mean, you said you like pie . . . I hoped you meant apple . . ."

She knew she was rambling. She watched him search his short-term memory for a mental file containing the key words, *"like pie."*

"You made us a pie?" he asked rather tenderly.

Felina reacted as if she had been pinched. "Wait. Are we an *us?*"

"Riiight . . . apples," he said, leaving Felina's question hanging. "It's coming back to me. You wanted the paper to see where they were on sale."

Mrs. W wondered if this utterance meant it was *all* coming back to him. His digital display in the hallway in particular. Particularly the part in Felina.

"What paper? What sale? Why are we talking about apples?" Felina looked back and forth between them as if they had some secret they were unpeeling together.

"I love apple pie," he said as if it was a prelude to an act of love.

He was up on his feet. He opened a cupboard door. He reached past her everyday dishes. He selected three hand painted fruit plates from the back. Mrs. W had brought them back from Brazil thirty years ago. They rarely came out of their hiding place. After attempts at drawer number one and drawer number two he had found the pewter pie slicer.

He cut artfully. Lifted three perfect pieces that still looked perfectly poised on the plate.

"No. Thank you." Mrs. W waved her plate away. "I don't want any."

"Yes, you do," José said. It was part insight, part command.

Felina hadn't waited for a fork. She had already begun. "Ummm . . . oh, it's so good. Oh, my God!" She was having one of her peak finger experiences.

Mrs. W thought she had noticed everything about José, but it intrigued her that he held his fork with a certain skill. European style. He ate with the respectful concentration of a judge at a food competition.

Slow. Reserved. As if his tongue was identifying every ingredient.

This act of savoring had Mrs. W's pulse quickening. She hoped he didn't notice the fork in her hand shaking. She put it on the table.

"Is that a dash of Li Hing Powder?"

Mrs. W, impressed at his culinary sophistication, could only nod.

"An intriguing finish," he added, savoring before swallowing another bite. "Balances the pallet. Awakens the mouth."

"I love it when you say things like "Awakens the mouth," Felina said.

"Don't you want it?" José said to Mrs. W who hadn't tasted her own pie.

Felina awakened from her pie-gasm to realize there were

two other people in the room.

José handed Mrs. W her fork. It was an instruction. She took it.

"Yes, she wants it." José took the liberty of answering for Mrs. W.

It was then that Felina noticed how Mrs. W couldn't take her eyes off of José and how his briefest gaze sent her feathers all a fluttering.

"Mrs. W! Looks like my man has your dough rising."

José's eyes met Felina's slow crooked smile as if this was the signal for some kind of slightly kinky game to begin.

"Guess you better be kneeding some dough." Felina was on her feet. Whatever this was, was already fun to her. "I'll be back," she said with the perfect tone of feminine mystique.

"Why?" Was all Mrs. W could muster.

"I have to feed my goldfish," she answered. She looked back at José just once, and left, closing the door behind her.

And all of a sudden Mrs. W was alone with the most dangerous—nearly naked, unshaven, man she had ever known—and he was sitting at her kitchen table.

With the creamy outline of him on her mauve tablecloth between them.

José didn't seem to notice that Mrs. W's heart beat could be heard across the street.

He silently finished his pie.

The clock ticked hideously. Taunting them for the lack of small talk.

Mrs. W felt moisture everywhere on her body.

Finally he put his fork down. He carried the Brazilian

dessert plates to the sink. His eyes turned to her.

She shivered.

Then—like a jolt of lightning—his arm pushed everything out of his way. He lifted her up onto the table. Right on top of his image.

His fervent lips tasted like sweet pie. His arms were strong. His desire was stronger.

He ripped open her robe. Checked her eyes. Eyes that wanted him.

"You know I'm going to give it to you," he said in a wet whisper near her ear.

"Yes," was the last word she could remember saying.

And that was the day Mrs. W found her smile.

The Kiss on the Bench
Sholmes

With headphones snug under her toque and music blaring she didn't hear his approach and, startled, jumped up from the bench when she saw him. There in that dark vacant park she usually saw no one. It was the reason she went there, alone at night, to smoke in secret. She often turned up in the spring and summer to swing unobserved as well. That way nobody could laugh at the whimsy of a 50 year old woman swinging in a child's playground by herself. Of course she knew he lived close by and often fantasized they would meet there but never once in five years had that happened. She yanked her iPod from her pocket and pressed stop. He was already talking and she missed some of it.

". . . mean to scare you," he was saying.

"It's OK," she managed. "My own fault. Not paying attention."

"Mind if I sit?"

"Knock yourself out," she countered, waving her arm in the direction of the bench with a nonchalance she was grateful to be able to summon, considering the exact opposite was true. She sat back down as he did. This may be the moment she'd been fantasizing about. This may be when the truth, as she concocted it, actually came from his lips. This may be but she'd be damned if confessions were going to spill from her mouth first. In case she was wrong.

For years now she had analyzed their every encounter ad nauseam. Trying to read his signals, if they really were signals, had occupied much of her time. Being neighbours meant they saw one another often on the street. Admittedly, only to her own self though, she stalked him a little. Knowing he would be driving to work at a specific ungodly hour, she would time her morning walk to pass him and they would wave and smile. Knowing he may walk his dog at a certain time, she planned her own errands to coincide. Is that what he would discuss with her, while sitting here on the bench?

Operating on the assumption that most men were thick, Sandra figured he would never see their frequent meetings as contrived. But sometimes she felt real fear. She often wondered if she was too obvious and if he would consider her some kind of threat. On occasion she had backed right off and purposely avoided being in his path just to take the heat off in case he thought her an interloper—if he thought of her at all. But soon she'd be back on that route, needing her fix of him, unable to help herself. She couldn't read his mind but offending him or causing him to avoid her was the last thing she wanted. The first thing she wanted was so inappropriate she was loathe to say it out loud. Patience was a not a virtue she possessed, but she sat silently waiting for him to speak.

"Come here often?" He smiled.

Was he considering his words as a bar-pick-up-line? She had no time to analyze it. "Actually I do," Sandra answered. "You?"

"Not much since the kids grew up," Charlie replied. "But I

saw you go down the path." He hesitated.

Choosing his words? Probably she was only imagining his attraction for her was as intense as hers was for him. It was all she could do to stay quiet.

"I thought maybe we could talk."

Oh no, Sandra thought, here it comes. Was he going to remind her that he's a married man or happily the father of three almost grown boys? Would he accuse her of jeopardizing his marriage, his happiness, his life? Would he see her as a desperate housewife and demand she cease and desist? She held her breath and braced herself for the onslaught. Clearly she deserved his contempt and had placed herself right in line for it. Slowly letting out her breath, she chirped in her friendliest whatever-could-you-wanna-talk-about voice, "Sure."

Charlie looked at his boots, squirmed in his seat and wrung his gloved hands.

He's nervous, Sandra noted, and her lack of patience won out. An actress she was not but she tried to sound innocuous.

"Was there something you wanted to say, Charlie?"

He turned his face to hers. From the glow of the moonlight she looked into his eyes and he into hers. There was a satisfying stop-time silence as neither spoke and neither averted their gaze. Sandra began a slow climb to hope.

This was not the first time they had shared such a stare. In the past it had always been Sandra's own guilty conscience that caused her to be the first to break the connection. Determined to know the truth, she held fast to his gaze. Looking into the face she saw day after day, she questioned for the millionth time what it was that attracted her. His teeth were crooked and discoloured in places. His chin was covered in grey, two day old stubble. His hair was thinning and in need of a cut. There was something though, something that had unnerved her those past five years.

The awkward silence grew loud in her ears. Impatiently she tried to think of something to say, to nudge him into a confession, to allay her own shameful position. Thankfully he found his voice.

"Do you ever think about me?" he whispered. "I mean . . . apart from just running in to me on the street now and then?"

Now and then was a gross understatement as it was practically a daily occurrence. Flashing through her brain on fast forward came the hundreds of times she sat on her porch reading, scanning the traffic for his car, watching from her office window for the dog that would signal its master was just a few yards behind so she could dash for the door as if she was coincidentally going out at the same time. Other times, slowing her pace as she neared their street, knowing she had not yet seen him on his morning commute so she must be early. Does she ever think about him? She thought of little else.

"Only in the most inappropriate ways." Sandra laughed. It was her nature to be flirty and friendly and sometimes a little outrageous. There was no point in being different now and she had rehearsed that line a million times in case he ever asked that question. Could they really, finally, be having this conversation?

He averted his eyes and then looked down at his boots. Why he was asking terrified her. If it was to make her stop seeking him out then her humiliation would be the least of her worries. It would be ironic to engage in an uncomfortable avoidance of one another without the memory of a steamy affair to accompany it. In other words, she'd get the punishment without committing the crime. If their daily wave on the street was all this was ever going to be—so be it—but she'd hate to not have even that just because she was making him anxious.

Part of her blamed his guilt at feeling the same way about her, but of course there was no way for her to know how he felt —unless he told her. Though she had had numerous opportunities to explain her feelings, she never had. The first move needed to be his and after all this time she had nearly given up. God knows she had assumed and surmised and projected how he must feel long enough. It was time to get to the truth—one way or the other. Sandra had a healthy respect for the difference between wanting something and having it. She hoped he wouldn't dismiss or detest her for even the mere suggestion that he was some kind of cheating dog. She needed to weigh her words. The silence had gone on too long. "Charlie?"

Charlie raised his eyes to hers again, their depth almost overwhelming. She could see his struggle and finally she knew. She leaned forward and pressed her lips to his, nudging them open with her tongue and in seconds their breathing became erratic. The kiss was gloriously hot and proved to her that the sexual chemistry was not just hers. Frantically their lips and tongues clashed and met and clashed again. Fire flames licked them both. The kiss went on and on. Sandra was delirious. And then, abruptly, it stopped. Caught off guard Sandra sat—mouth open wide in mid kiss. Charlie rose from the bench, gave her a short shamefaced peek and ran up the path out of the park.

* * *

Sandra snuggled in close to the warm arm wrapped around her naked body. His other hand slid down her back and paused a moment to caress her bum.

"Nice ass," he breathed into her ear as his fingers moved even lower, prompting her body to respond. She wasn't disappointed. Sandra loved sex, everything about it, and she gave herself up to the pleasure. Her body was made for this, she thought, and her husband was the best lover she'd ever known. Years of practice together had made their sex life phenomenal. She trusted him completely and over the years had succumbed to every kinky act he wanted to try. She knew he would never hurt her and she knew he could always please her. Even she was shocked at some of the things they'd tried—and liked—no loved. This morning was no exception. Her orgasm left her breathless and spent.

"Wanna join me in the shower dirty girl?" he teased as he roused himself out of her and off the bed.

Shaking her head, Sandra snuggled back into the pillows and Michael shrugged his shoulders. "You don't know what you're missing baby." He smirked and padded out of the bedroom to the adjoining bath.

She lay there thinking of Michael, thinking of Charlie, wondering what the hell she was thinking.

Consciously pushing Charlie from her mind, Sandra tried to focus on her real life. On her husband and son, the love they shared, the life they built. For 20 years Michael had been her lover, friend, supporter and confidante. He was the best thing that ever happened to a torn up girl who didn't believe in love. After a father who wasn't content just to abandon her emotionally but had to strike the point hard with beatings and abuse, Sandra believed love was an elusive lie fabricated by philosophers trying to explain the meaning of life. She never wanted to marry, never wanted children, never knew that a family could be like the one she had now and yet, even though she certainly had it, real love still seemed implausible.

Sandra had an innate ability to separate love from sex. They were not mutually inclusive and never had been. At times love had gotten in the way of sex and messed it up. She had left several men because they insisted on loving her when she just wanted their physical presence. That's how she thought of Charlie—physically. She had no longing to be his second wife, or his mistress. She did not want a divorce. She just, yes, selfishly, wanted to fuck him. Would he be able to isolate the two? Not likely. Most people—married people—could not!

The other side of that argument was Michael. Though she believed a tryst with Charlie would not change her feelings towards her husband, she did realize that he deserved to be honoured, and cheating on him was just wrong. He might leave her if he found out. There was no question that Michael leaving her was the worst thing that could happen. Sandra really couldn't imagine her life without him. He took such good care of her and he loved her very much. Still her mind kept drifting to the kiss on the bench.

* * *

"This is ridiculous." Sandra threw the brush back into the drawer. Five times she had tried to fix her bed-head to no avail. Most mornings she just brushed her teeth and left. Some days, when she particularly felt the earliness of her exercise hour she might wash her face. But today she was concerned about her appearance. She even dabbed on a little make-up. She wished Charlie had lost his battle with temptation a few years ago before her hysterectomy and menopause had added ten jiggly pounds to her abdomen. She stood sideways to the mirror and groaned at the extra bulk. Sure, her skin and face were still attractive and everyone said she didn't look close to 50 but the confidence she exuded with her lovely slim body even a couple of years ago was gone. How could she think to let someone other than Michael see this old, worn-out body? Thankfully most of it would be hidden under her ski jacket. Man. It was getting late. She had to go.

Sandra was certain that today's morning walk would be life-changing. Today was the day Charlie would stop on his commute. She felt it, she envisioned it, and she wanted it. In all those years, even though she had trumped up many ridiculous reasons why he might, he had never once stopped. But that was before the kiss on the bench.

Desperate Measures by Marianas Trench blared in Sandra's ears as she pushed the walk button at the Stephanie Road intersection. Her tummy had been flop-flipping since Gordon Street. IF she were to see Charlie, Stephanie Road was the place he would be. Casually she scanned the paltry number of cars on the road at such an ungodly hour. Good for a secret rendezvous she thought and her stomach not only flopped but belched a fart. Geez, she was as nervous as a cat in water. What if he drove right by? Maybe he wouldn't even wave. Maybe he chose an alternate route to avoid her. Maybe . . .

There he was!

Charlie's mini van was parked on Stephanie just past the intersection. His headlights blinked off and on. Sandra turned off her music and walked directly to the driver's window. She was guilt ridden and nervous, and likely he was too, but after all this time she was euphoric. One way or another she would get her answers. She crossed her fingers and prayed he wasn't waiting to tell her no.

"You wanna get in a minute?" Charlie whispered and jerked his head in the direction of the passenger door.

Sandra didn't hesitate. "Yes," she breathed and yanked open the driver's door. His surprise did not deter her. She climbed and straddled his lap in one fluid motion. Before he could even react, Sandra unzipped her jacket, placed her arms around his neck and drew him in for a kiss. Again the kiss was one of sexual excitement shared by two. His hands touched her shoulders and tugged at her jacket sleeves. She released his neck so her coat could slide off and plopped her hands on his chest inside his already unbuttoned coat. The kiss continued in its frantic, can-hardly-get-enough way, while his hands moved to her teeny breasts supported only by her tight workout T shirt. She knew her nipples jutted out from the chill in the van. Had they enticed him on her many a cool morning walks? It felt as wonderful as all her imaginings had led her to believe it would. Charlie kneaded her breasts like pizza dough, all the while moving his tongue around the inside of her mouth in unison with her own. Shoving her T shirt up over her breasts he broke off their kiss and bent his head to take one gaping nipple into his mouth. Sandra writhed, groaning her desire. Placing her hand behind his head she pulled him closer into her body. She wanted this—all of it—and it seemed that he did too. Reluctant to stop for even a moment, Sandra rose from his lap and jumped the console. "Join me back here," she breathed and leapt into the bench seat. Charlie followed without hesitation. With some room to move, Sandra caressed his crotch through his jeans and was rewarded by moans of pleasure. Unbuckling his belt proved impossible so he did it, and released his top button and unzipped. Sandra shucked her jacket and pulled her T-shirt over her head and off with lightening speed.

He resumed his sucking, and his hand found its way into her leggings. Sandra pulled in her stomach, aware of its girth and more than a little self-conscious, but soon forgot about it as his finger moved inside her. Having wanted this for so long, she was dripping already.

"Ahhh," she whimpered and snaked her hand inside his pants. His cock was rock hard and pleasingly large. She caressed it, moving her hands up and down and around until neither of them could stand it another minute.

"I've wanted this for soooo long," Charlie's breathy, rapid whisper confirmed her hopes. With conciliatory silence they broke apart and hastily removed the clothing barriers. Assuming he would enter her now, Sandra spread her legs, but Charlie bowed his head to her Y and licked her pussy lips. Over and over his tongue licked and pulled and pushed at her snatch. It was arousing, and heady, and so wrong and so spectacular. Time meant nothing. Sandra didn't know if they'd been that way for five minutes or five hours and she cried out when he stopped. But Charlie wasn't finished yet. He kissed her big belly and left a trail of saliva all the way up her body, stopping briefly at her breasts before claiming her mouth again. Sandra was hot. She wanted him so bad. Gently he directed her head to his penis and she gobbled it up. Running her tongue around the bottom of the mushroom top (just the way Michael liked it) had him gasping and panting. Taking it completely in her mouth and then out and then in, ten, twenty, thirty times made him cry out her name. Finally she stopped and positioned herself on top of him. His head was leaning back against the rest and his eyes were closed. Not deterred, she slid over his cock with ease. She was wet and burning and ready. Slowly she pumped up and down and when she was sure it was all feeling the way it should, she sped up to a frenzied pace. His hands grabbed her waist, helping her momentum, up and down, over and over. She watched his features, distorted with pleasure until his eyes finally opened wide in ecstasy. Taking from him the orgasm that she had fantasized about for years, Sandra closed her eyes to let the fulfilment wash over her.

Finally satiated, they lay still. Sandra's head rested on Charlie's shoulder. She was afraid to look at him, terrified to see the regret and remorse that could so easily follow this heinous indiscretion. Neither of them spoke or even moved for what seemed like an eternity.

"That was exactly as I imagined it would be," he whispered, stroking her head.

"Me too," she replied, meeting his eyes. He kissed her with less passion this time but with just as much unbridled desire. They retrieved their clothes and dressed in silence. Sandra thought about Charlie being late for work and about what she would tell Michael about her own tardiness. She couldn't help but wonder what would happen next.

Charlie, now dressed, opened the side van door and reached for her hand, helping her out.

"I can't do this again you know." He said it with such reluctance that Sandra's heart skipped a beat.

"I know," she replied. And she did know. Engaging in an ongoing affair simply would not work. That's how you got caught. All the lies and deceptions necessary would be impossible to sustain without discovery. Inevitably they'd end up in divorce court. Charlie was right. Sandra was right. This one time was all they could have. Grabbing her iPod, Sandra fiddled to get her music working and raised her other hand to wave good bye. Charlie stilled her wave, placed both his hands over hers and said, "So, see ya tomorrow morning?"

"Tomorrow," said Sandra and skip walked the rest of the way home.

"I think older women still have a full life."
Betty White

Harvest
MZina

You enter me like an arrow.
To the roots of your tree
I am soil.

No rocks or frozen tundra here.
Yielding my ground is, soft
as powdered snow.

Plant in me.
Your strong hand,
your muscled back,
your weathered face.

A farmer with a heart of gold.

BANANA

Who can see a banana
Without thinking of other things.
The imagination leaps about
The libido takes to wing.

So peel one back and have a go
And like Deep Throat's reputation.
Enjoy a healthy snack or two
And enhance your recreation!

The Hell with Martinique
Delia Hammond

He was the most magnificent creature she had ever even imagined, sitting on the hillside like an Olympian God.

Cassy, in Antigua for the annual race week, sailed with a group of friends as part of an all women crew. Although they had never won anything of any consequence, during the races they always had a fabulous time, released from families, husbands, children, divorces and/or dead-end jobs. The last thing she expected was the appearance of such a gorgeous looking stud of a man.

The crew, seated before a makeshift stage and eager to hear the announcements of the winners of the various races, chatted with each other. The outdoor theatre on the lawns of the old Copper and Lumber Store, now a hotel in which Cassy had a room, was perfect for the closing festivities. The only minus was the gathering of an ominous cloud, which the audience eyed with trepidation.

Cassy had scanned for old friends from previous races she'd attended, when she spotted him on the hillside—dark curly hair, a physique worthy of the Chippendales, and even at this distance, eyes that matched the blue of his silk shirt. She had no idea how to manage an introduction at the post-awards reception. It had been eons since she had flirted with men or been bold enough to create her own "accidental meetings" with delicious males. Somehow crossing the forty barrier had stripped her confidence.

Without warning, a hailstone landed with a painful thump on Cassy's nose, followed by a deafening peal of thunder. Before she was able to comment to one of her crew members, a torrent of water, mixed with stinging ice pellets sent them scurrying for shelter.

She ran to her room to change and regretted she would probably never meet the stud since she needed to catch an early plane to Martinique for a week of evaluating yachts for sale. In four days, she would have to sound intelligent when she took a crucially important client to view the vessels she recommended.

Half an hour later, dry and warm, Cassy walked into the lobby—cum bar area—of the hotel to discover the others had invaded the bar instead of returning to their own hotels on the rest of the island. People were standing in groups, chatting and laughing. Evelyn, her roommate, waved a beckoning hand from across the room. In her other, she held aloft a large glass of punch.

On her way over, Cassy stopped and ordered a small white wine. She avoided rum because one drink of the "demon" stuff and she became randy as hell.

When she joined her friends, the announcer, still wet and soggy himself, tapped on the mike to attract the attention of the crowd, and proceeded to award prizes to the participants. At one point in the festivities, a well known, but rather inebriated local sailor, stepped up to bestow the prize for "fastest finish in a wooden boat."

Cassy giggled at his pronunciation of the name of the

winner, a man from Dubrovnik, and said, "That was all Greek to me."

"Ah, you speak Greek." The voice from behind her, deep and throaty, sounded like melted chocolate.

She turned with a start and stopped with her nose inches from the ultimate in boy-toy, stud-muffin, tangle-worthy, chest hair. The scent of clean soapy male drifted into her nostrils.

She blushed, stepped back, looked up and locked eyes with—the man from the hillside. He was no boy-toy, just hot juicy male, with eyes carved from summer skies, blue and shining and warmed by sun. The nose, the lips, ah, he had the face of a god sculpted by Michelangelo. His dark mass of black curls invited her fingers to comb them back from his eyes. She had to clench her fists to keep them at her sides. To her horror, she realized she had been staring at him, her mouth half open. Closing it with an almost audible snap, she stammered, "I only know how to say 'please' and 'thank you'."

He grinned at her. "That is all a woman needs to know."

His voice contained a hint of mischief, negating any possible offense.

Before the perfect comeback came to her mind, he rescued her with introductions to his crew. They smiled and welcomed her. He continued, "I am Stefan Kouros. I brought a new yacht to the races this year. She's a good one and we came in second in our class. I think we'll do better when the crew gets used to her."

He asked her name and smiled. "Cassy? In Greek mythology Kassandra was the daughter of a king. The name means a woman who entangles men. Should I worry about you Cassy? Are you going to entangle me?"

Her thoughts had become even more libidinous. *If I get the chance, you betcha!* Aloud she said, "No man gets entangled unless he wants to."

He just cocked an eyebrow and chuckled.

"You mentioned you bought a new yacht. What kind?"

"A Swan," he replied, "Her name is Nani."

"Nani sounds Hawaiian, not Greek."

"It is. I bought her from someone who admired Hawaiian names, and Nani means beautiful. A good name for a good yacht, and since it is very unlucky to change the name of a vessel, I kept it."

"Swans are beautiful. They are one of my favorites. Sublimely confident on the ocean, gorgeous to look at, and a dream to sail."

"You know boats?"

"I'm a yacht broker."

"That explains much. I think you should finish your drink, because I would like to feed you."

Cassy's eyebrows shot up.

"Dinner, I mean. We are going to celebrate with much food and many drinks, and I would be honored if you would join us. And, we can talk more about our mutual interest in . . . yachts." It was more suggestive than a simple discussion about boats.

"Thank you, I'd love to." Cassy almost batted her eyes. She couldn't believe at her age, not only was she acting like a horny teenager, but she was letting a man whom she'd only just met pick her up. His crew were staring at her. *Do they think it odd he's inviting me to become part of their group?*

Stefan must have seen them too, and announced, "They are only here as crew, and they are young, and don't know how to fully appreciate a beautiful woman."

Good grief, the man needs glasses! But who cares. If he thinks I'm beautiful, that's good enough for me.

* * *

At dinner in one of Antigua's best restaurants, she had the chance to examine him closely. Even with strands of gray in his hair she suspected he might still be her junior by a few years. She knew her face looked at least 15 years younger than her chronological age, but her body had softened, gained a a pound or two or three, and sagged a little over the past decade. *What if I have to get naked?*

Her divorce final, and with no other ties, why not sample this amazingly hot man who had dropped into her life with such explosive force. Warm thoughts and warmer feelings suffused her. She had thought sensitivities like this could not be rekindled. *Maybe naked might be worth it.*

Beneath the tablecloth his fingers brushed the top of her thigh. She didn't move away. A moment later they touched again, tracing flames and pausing at the wrong side of fulfillment. She wanted to grab his glorious hand and guide him further up where she was on fire and pulsing with need. Lordy, she wasn't just acting like a horny teenager. Except for her age, she was one.

He leaned across the table. "I think I should walk you home, don't you?" His breath warm with a faint scent of wine, enticed her further.

"Umm . . . well . . . yes."   She had forgotten she had to be at the airport at 6 am to catch her plane.

As they walked back to her hotel, Stefan's arm rested on her shoulder. Fingers caressed her ear and neck, gently stroking the top of her collar bone. A full moon was shining and in the light she wondered if he could detect her nipples springing to rigid attention. She ached for him touch her all over and shivered with the thought of his mouth at her breast.

"Which room is yours?" he asked.

"We can't go there, my roommate is asleep. What about your yacht?" *Good grief, I'm ready to bed this man! I've only just met him. Does that make me qualify as a "slut"?*

"Nani is full of crew for the next two days. No place on board is private right now."

A bereft Cassy heard only the birdlike calls of the tree frogs. All else was silent.

"Hmm, we are not doomed to frustration, because . . ." he pulled her into a small alcove in the hotel lobby, and pressing his lips to hers, sought the soft areas inside her mouth with his hot, eager tongue. He reached under her dress and grasped the top of her pants.

The fire within died, drenched by the reality of the scenario. "Wait," she ordered and pushed him away. "I'm not a 'knee-trembler in an alley' kind of woman."

He did a double take. "A what?"

Cassy blushed and mumbled, "A knee trembler."

"I have not heard the term before, but I can guess the meaning. I thought you wanted me as much as I want you?"

"This is too public. It is not comfortable and I can't."

"You are a woman who prefers a soft bed, dim lights, perhaps music? I understand. Tomorrow we plan. We will find what is available."

"Oh no," She said. "I have to go to Martinique in the morning."

"Why are you going to Martinique? And why tomorrow?"

"I have to spend four days looking at yachts. On Thursday, one of my best clients is coming over to buy one and it's my job to recommend the best."

"No problem. Tomorrow you will cancel your reservation, and the next morning we can sail over in Nani." His smile was self-satisfied. "I will help you find a yacht for this customer. I am good at finding good yachts."

"But . . ."

"No but. Tomorrow we will breakfast in town and discuss this. I will meet you here in the morning."

He closed his mouth over her, stopping further protests. The flames were hotter than ever. Cassy grabbed his curls to hold him to her. He was almost arrogant ordering her around, but he was Greek and incredibly confident. Mostly he was so hot, she was able to forgive him anything. As she leaned into him, the physical evidence of his desire was obvious.

He disentangled her fingers from his hair and shook his head at her. "Be careful Miss Kassandra, you are playing with fire, and if you do not release me . . . it could be dangerous."

She pouted and mused to herself, *Wow, I thought I'd forgotten how to pout.* "I am not Kassandra. I was christened Cassy"

He laughed, kissed his finger and pressed it to her lips,

"You are more than you know, and much more than I expected."

He turned, and disappeared into the night.

Sleep was impossible. Erotic dreams plagued Cassy, bringing her to consciousness as waking thoughts crowded with images of Stefan and those magic hands. Men's hands fascinated her. Big strong ones conjured up visions of submission to satisfy insatiable desires. She clutched her pillow to her, but the darn thing refused to take his place.

At 5 am the buzzer sounded. She groaned, whacked the alarm into silence, rolled over, and buried her head in her faithless pillow. It wouldn't hurt to delay her flight. She brightened. *Yes! Breakfast with Stefan*! *That alone might be worth one day less in Martinique.*

Lazy, sexy thoughts of a day with him, occupied her until her roommate Evelyn woke and looked over at Cassy in surprise.

"I thought you had to catch a plane?"

"I did. I'm going tomorrow instead."

"Am I to understand the blue-eyed god is responsible for this change of mind?"

"Yeah, sort of."

Evelyn laughed. "Adorable men always interfere with women's plans, don't they? Well, I'm off to St John's for the day. I'll see you tonight, unless of course, you're out with the fabulous bod."

* * *

With perfect timing, Cassy came down the stairs just as Stefan entered the hotel. Smiling broadly, he crossed the lobby and unexpectedly, greeted her with a kiss. Surprised, she had no time to pucker properly and almost banged noses with him. They laughed.

It's going to be a good day.

Breakfast was just the beginning of a day to be long remembered. Stefan took her to parts of the island unknown to her, yet she had sailed these waters for five years. They stood, looking over a cove she had not seen before.

"The pirates are said to have buried treasure in the cave below these cliffs," he said. "But it is usually below water and the waves are fierce on this side of the island. Scuba diving is most unwise in this cove."

"Do you scuba dive too?"

"I used to. As a child in Greece, I could never get deep enough to see everything just by free-diving. With an air tank, you can look at so many treasures."

"Why don't you dive any more?"

"A man has to grow up, and when I had a wife and children, I became more cautious."

"You . . . you're married?"

"Not for many years. But I never regained my passion for diving."

"I'm sorry to hear that, but how do you know all this about Antigua?"

"I've been coming here for more than ten years. I used to own a villa not far from here. Too bad I sold it last year. Last night could have been spent in comfort." He touched her arm. "Is your roommate still at the hotel?"

"Yes, she doesn't leave for New York until Thursday

morning."

"Another too bad. My crew are also here until tomorrow and I checked for space at every hotel. Because of race week, all rooms are booked."

"I'm going to live through another sleepless night," she grumbled.

"Pardon?"

"Nothing, its just . . ."

"I know, Kassandra. I too wish for something better for us."

"I'm not Kassandra. My name is Cassy."

"No, you are definitely Kassandra, and I believe I am becoming entangled." He leaned over and kissed her softly behind her left ear, and then, cupping her chin, brought her mouth to his.

Without thinking, her arms were around him and she melted into the embrace, attempting to be one body. Time did not stand still, but flowed around them thick and lazy like sweet molasses.

Someone was calling her name and she sprang away from him. She looked up to see Evelyn walking toward them with a devilish smile on her face. *Damn, she'd seen them groping each other.*

"I thought that was you," Evelyn said. "We had a fabulous day in St. John's and I bought out all the shops. I even had to buy an extra suitcase to take everything home. By the way, this is Judy and her husband Sam. They're friends of mine living on the island. We were just on our way to dinner at The Saint James Club. Would you like to join us? Tuesday is lobster night. Yum."

"A most enjoyable suggestion. Thank you, we'd love to." Stefan accepted before Cassy had a chance to object.

Evelyn continued. "Our reservations are in half an hour, so we'll just be able to make it on time. You have car? Do you know how to get there?"

Stefan nodded 'yes' to both questions. "We will follow you shortly," he said, "we just need to pick up a package we left at the shop down the hill."

* * *

In the car, on the way to dinner Cassy demanded, "Why did you accept? We could have gone somewhere more secluded and romantic, even though we can't find a room."

"You worry too much," he said. "I am a member of the Saint James Club in London, and just perhaps, for me they might find a room."

"I thought you lived in Greece?"

"I do, and sometimes I live in Monaco, but I often go to London on business so I spend time there as well. It is logical to belong to the club so I can get accommodation at the last minute."

She laughed with delight and threw her arms around him. The car swerved and he stopped to avoid running off the road. The two of them touched and kissed and stroked each other until they were both hot and panting.

"For god's sake woman, desist. I only have so much control, and you do not do the 'knee-tremblings,' right?"

"Knee tremblers," she corrected, but heeded the warning.

She would have to wait until the availabilities at the club were unearthed. Allowing the tiniest of smiles, she thought to herself, *I am trembling though, and my knees most of all.*

* * *

No rooms were available for the entire week. Cassy was devastated.

"Sometimes, waiting increases the final pleasure," he said.

She sensed he was also disappointed and all she managed was, "Hmph," as they made their way to the dining room.

The maitre d' led them to the table where Evelyn and her friends were already into their first cocktails.

"The lobster dinners here are amazing," Evelyn said. "Whenever I hit Antigua, dinner at Saint James is a necessity."

She was right. Cassy's lobster was a good three pounds, but was perfectly cooked and sweet and juicy. Dipped in drawn butter, it was ambrosia to the tongue and even at the very "upper crusty" Saint James, they were given bibs, which was a good thing. She felt butter dripping down her chin, but before she managed to mop it up, Stefan's finger wiped her face. Then he put his finger between his lips and sucked on it.

Cassy's mouth was dry as she stared at his hands. Her imagination ran wild, creating turmoil in her body. The flush begin at her neck and travelled up to set her cheeks aflame.

Stefan just grinned knowingly at her. *How was she every going to make it through this night without losing her mind?*

With lobsters demolished, deserts sampled, and relaxing with a heady, intoxicating balloon of cognac, the conversation returned to sailing. Each had their favorite locations and Cassy discovered Stefan, like her, enjoyed the Leewards the most. The best island debate surged on, but Stefan's hands, out of sight of the others, were relentless. She found concentrating on the topic almost impossible.

Evelyn's voice broke through the haze of lust. "By the way, Cassy, I decided to delay my trip to New York. Judy and Sam invited me to sail for a couple of days over to Saint Barts. My bags are already on board, but I kept the room for another night because I know you're not leaving 'til tomorrow." Evelyn smirked at her.

Cassy swallowed, and replied as calmly as she was able. "Thanks, I appreciate it."

She clutched Stefan's thigh in excitement. Tonight they'd have a room.

He barely winced and pried off the fingers digging into him. Cassy glanced at him apologetically. She'd forgotten her wrists were strong from winding winches so many years.

Cutting short the post dinner liqueurs, they made their excuses and left for the old Copper and Lumber Store.

Stefan laughed. "You see? Sometimes you just have to be patient. Perhaps we met so I can teach you to take life as it comes and not fight circumstances." He looked at her, his eyes tender, "And you can teach me what I have forgotten about passion.

* * *

The brief ride in the car seemed interminable. They were unable to keep their hands off each other.

Stefan parked and they hurried into the hotel, bumping hips and grabbing kisses without pausing in their pursuit of privacy.

Cassy reached into her purse, pulled out the keychain, and in her haste dropped it. She grabbed it off the floor and tried inserting the key into the lock, without success. Stefan calmly took the key from her, turned it over, and handed it back to her. She slid it in and at last the entrance to her room yielded.

Stefan kicked the door shut behind them, his mouth exploring and tasting hers, his lips firm, demanding, yet gentle. He drew back, and with his tongue, softly outlined her lips. Just as she considered screaming for mercy, he transferred his attention to her neck and ears, distributing light touches which set off a thousand small explosions of ecstasy.

He pulled the zipper down her back and her dress slithered down her body and pooled on the floor. He slid one bra strap over her shoulder and carefully planted kisses along her collar bone. When he moved the other strap he switched to the hollow in her throat. She was besotted and bewildered and past all practical thought. She forced herself to slowly undo each of the buttons of his shirt to expose a mass of glorious crisp curly hair. She ran her fingers through the tangles as his body pressed against her. Strong, alive, and scorching hot.

He scooped her up in his arms and carried her to the bed. Barely able to contain herself, she reached for his zipper.

He put his hand over hers. "Slow down," he said. "Time extends the pleasure. You are pushing me too close to the edge."

He leisurely removed his belt and shorts and sat astride her. Unhurriedly, he began kissing her belly, inserting his tongue in her navel. The sensation was exquisite. Reaching underneath her with one hand he unsnapped her bra. *How did he do that?*

He lowered his head to her breast to place hot, wet kisses on her turgid nipples and unbidden she grabbed handfuls of his curls. They were like soft lamb's wool, but the exquisite ministrations of his mouth held her attention. Heat built in her lower body. Desperate for him to fill her, she reached down for him again.

"Slowly," he said again, stopping her hands in their quest.

He traced hot kisses down her belly and when he removed her lacy underwear, she gasped with delight as his tongue encouraged newfound desires. No one had ever pleasured her this way. The passion built, with light and sound and color combined to an explosion of . . . of . . . shudders throughout her body of the most incredible sensations.

He paused and slowly removed his underwear.

"Stefan don't stop. Please, don't stop."

His eyes filled with passion as he moved over her and with deep thrusts, brought this most extraordinary pleasure to a screaming conclusion.

Cassy fell back exhausted, and, aware of her less-than-perfect body, reached for a sheet to cover herself.

Stefan stopped her hand. "No. I want to look at you. You are a beautiful woman, Kassandra. You have bewitched and entangled me so I am no longer a sane man."

She almost stopped breathing. *I guess I am a Kassandra. And, with him, I do feel beautiful.*

He stroked her bare skin. They were lazy seductive fondles, but stirrings in hidden places raised their heads attentively.

She moaned. She wanted more. The addictive passion suffused her and she wriggled seductively. "Again?" she asked, licking her lips suggestively.

He smiled, his eyes still veiled with the aftermath of their exertions. "You are insatiable. I will probably die of too much lovemaking." However, his fingers reached down to buried treasures. She had her answer.

Obligations faded fast, and she spared but a brief thought of her customer waiting to view all those yachts.

The hell with Martinique.

"In Europe, we admire grown-up women; I think men revere older women."

Francesca Annis

The Church Bulletin
Amanda Townsend

Martha Canfield poured a second cup of Red Rose tea while she talked to her daughter on the phone. "I was in Chapters last week looking for a book on casseroles and saw that Fifty Shades book that everyone's talking about."

"You didn't buy one, did you?" said Caroline.

"No. I don't need a book to tell me fifty ways to cover my gray hair. And why is a man's tie on the cover?"

"Mom, that book is not about hair colour. I'm in a rush. Gotta go."

"And I have to get to my writing. Bye." Martha hung up, picked up her tea and walked down the hall to Caroline's old bedroom—now a craft and writing room. As much as she tried to keep her activities separate, balls of wool or a yard of fabric habitually strayed to the writing side. She put her tea on the desk and removed a gargantuan ball of mauve yarn from Charlie's ancient Smith Corona. Caroline called the typewriter a dinosaur and had offered to buy her a computer. Martha had tried one out but missed the friendly clatter of keys, and the church secretary didn't mind scanning the typed pages of her monthly contribution to the Church Bulletin.

After Charlie died, the pastor suggested she write a couple of paragraphs to add a personal touch to the usual marriage, birth and death notices, and for the past eleven years, she had religiously provided a short folksy story or inspiring vignette.

Time to write. She sharpened three yellow pencils, lined them up beside two pens and a bottle of Wite-Out, and straightened a stack of typing paper. All ready to create.

She took a sip of tea and gazed out the window. Last night's heavy snowfall left ghostly blobs along side streets and over back lawns. She could hear the rhythmic scrape of Mr. Gunther's shovel, two houses away. After shoveling his own walk, he would do hers. It was nice to have someone shovel for her, but he was beginning to get a bit too friendly, like insisting she call him Arnold.

Martha turned back to the Smith Corona. *What should I write for February's insertion?*

Just then Mopsy, Topsy and Sam, three kittens she was fostering, tottered into the room. She plucked a ball of fire engine red from the basket of wool at her feet and tossed it toward the trio. Sam pounced first, following quickly by his sisters who threw themselves into the fray to bring down the writhing monster.

Martha fed a piece of paper into the typewriter, placed her fingers on the home row and typed: *Three Little Kittens.* Corny, but she could change it later. Her knowing fingers tap-danced over the keys, not stopping for corrections on this first draft. Halfway down, she stopped typing, closed her eyes and waited. Nothing. She looked up and studied the fleur-de-lis relief on the ceiling. Music might coax the reluctant muse. She rolled her chair across the room to the CD player. Mr. Gunther—Arnold— had given her Wagner's *Tristan and Isolde* for Christmas, saying it was his favourite opera and she just *had* to hear it. She put in the last disc and rolled back to her typewriter.

The music rose in steady crescendos, getting higher and higher. The soaring sounds overlapped the scrape of Arnold's shovel as the chords swelled and overflowed the room, filling her body with tremulous notes.

Her fingers took off, pounding on the keys, as if belonging to someone else. The steady clattering beat a gush of letters onto the page. Syllables grew into words and words into sentences as line followed line. She typed so quickly, her eyes couldn't keep up with the blur rushing across the paper. Flying fingertips leapt over keys, racing in time to the rising notes of music. Her scalp tingled as the carbon ribbon whirled out row after row of streaming sentences.

She pulled the first sheet out and wound in another. Tumbling, crashing words filled the page and she grasped the top edge and yanked, making the platen rattle. On the third page, lively fingers resumed their frantic mission. Half way down the page, Wagner stopped with a rousing climax and on the final note, with one swift finger, she hit the exclamation key.

Her heart beat overtime. She slapped her hand to her chest to slow her breathing just as the scraping shovel arrived at the front of her house. Arnold would be knocking on her door when he was finished. *What was she going to do with him? She had only known one man all her life and for the last few years before he died they had been more like brother and sister. Was she too old for another man?* Arnold was so insistent. And still in good shape for sixty-five. She shook her head. Enough of that nonsense. She was done with men and all that stuff.

She turned back to her typewriter, cranked the last piece of paper out and placed it upside down on the desk on top of the first two pages. A fresh cup of tea was what she needed while she read her masterpiece. She dodged the three fur balls, still trouncing the wet and shredded mass of wool, and returned a few minutes later with a cup of Earl Grey. She picked up the first sheet. *The congregation will love this story about three darling kittens and their romp with a wayward ball of red wool.*

She laughed at the first few sentences about how they pulled the wool apart, tangling themselves up. Such a rollicking time. Halfway down the page, she frowned and read the next sentence twice.

Did she write this? Well, of course. Who else? But she couldn't have. This part wasn't about kittens. It was about a woman named Kitten. And—oh my! What *was* she doing?

She couldn't have written this. She would *never* write such words about . . .

A patch of heat crept up the back of her neck, growing hotter with each line. She drew in a sharp breath and clasped a hand to her bosom. This could never be printed in the church bulletin. This was a tale of a mature woman, a Miss Kitty, about Martha's own age. She had long silver gray hair, and she was disrobing in front of a young man named Arnold. *Arnold?*

Her hands shook as she read on.

"Miss Kitty pushed a tight fitting black skirt down over her voluptuous hips. She peeled off a pink cashmere sweater, uncovering two heaving mounds of pulsating flesh, half hidden by a lacy bra. Arnold squirmed in the arm chair in which he was seated. His wrists were bound with a crimson drapery cord to the carved arms of the chair."

Outrageous!

"Miss Kitty, in red spike heels . . ."

So impractical

". . . turned, showing her perfect peach of a backside barely concealed by silk white panties."

This woman was a showoff, exposing her underwear to this Arnold fellow. If you could call bikini panties and a lacy bra that hardly covered anything, underwear. She should stop reading.

"Miss Kitty stroked her hands over her body. She cupped her breasts and massaged them with slow circular movements. Then she pushed her splayed fingers over her rounded tummy and into the waste band of her bikini panties. Her nail polish matched her red spike heels. She lifted her eyebrows, withdrew one hand and placed it on the top of her left thigh. Then she spread her fingers and scraped her hand up her leg while licking her lips with a luscious tongue."

And Arnold is watching all of this. She absolutely must stop reading now.

The second sheet glared at her, daring her to pick it up. Surely this one would be about kittens playing with a ball of wool. She gingerly plucked the corner with her thumb and index finger.

"Miss Kitty writhed and postured in front of Arnold. She stuck a saucy hip forward and turned to show her peachy backside. Arnold was . . ."

Oh my word!

". . . nude except for a grey tie—a long grey tie that hung down to his lap covering his privates."

Well, I should think so.

"His body was muscular and strong. Sweat trickled down his forehead and moisture beaded over his top lip. His ankles were also tied so he couldn't even move his feet to roll the office chair forward. Miss Kitty moved closer, swaying like a belly dancer and, when she got six inches from him, she lowered her head and swept her long silver hair over his face and down his chest. Arnold strained toward her, stretching his neck and tongue, trying to touch her hot flesh."

Martha held the paper tighter, willing herself to breath.

"Miss Kitty moved her pulsing breasts closer—an inch away—and then pulled back. With a sly smile, she cupped her hands under them, and held them up to him. He poked his head forward and stretched out his tongue, but couldn't reach the delectable titbit. She moved her hands down to a tilted hip, and thigh and . . ."

Oh, dear.

". . . inserted two fingers up between her legs.

Arnold groaned. 'Untie me, pleeeease . . .'

She laughed. 'Not yet,' she said, and slid her fingers in and out of herself, while licking her lips with a moist tongue."

Would she untie him? She won't read any more. Outside, the real Arnold scraped a steady beat with his snow shovel, moving closer and closer to her front door.

"Miss Kitty, still in her blood red stilettos, sauntered around the back of Arnold's chair. She grabbed his head and buried it between her hot mounds. Pushing her breasts against the top of his graying hair, she stroked his damp forehead. Then she bent over and licked his ear, tickling it with her tongue."

Oh, dear heaven. Martha grabbed a tissue and wiped her brow.

"Arnold moaned and twisted his body side to side and up and down. His tie shifted a bit, but still covered his jewels."

Charlie never called his private parts, jewels.

"Miss Kitty laughed and stuck her index finger into his mouth. She withdrew it slowly, letting it linger over his quivering bottom lip before she pulled it out. Then she sashayed toward a three-paneled Japanese screen in front of him. As she walked away, her back to him, she unhooked her bra and flicked it at him. It landed on his lap, one cup draped over his right knee. She stepped behind the screen. A moment later, a pair of white panties flipped over the top edge."

The brazen hussy.

"A rustle and Miss Kitty strolled out . . ."

Still in those impossible shoes.

". . . wearing a transparent negligee. Arnold's eyes darted to her dark triangular bush and to the swaying full breasts—nipples hard. The grey tie in his lap rose up and he yanked at his restraints.

'Please,' he cried. 'Untie me.'"

End of page two. Martha's hands trembled—her palms damp. She picked up the third page. Only half a page. *What can happen on half a page?*

"Miss Kitty ambled toward Arnold . . . closer . . . closer. She put a hand on each of his shoulders. Soft, flimsy material brushed his face and a breast hung a breath from his cheek.

Leaning back, she undid her top button . . . and the next one . . . and the next and all the way down to the last one. Her negligee swung open. She leaned forward, lifted Arnold's tie and lowered herself unto him."

Oh good gracious! She flung the paper away like a hot ember. It landed on her teacup. The paper dimpled and one edge curled up. She snatched it off and it floated to the floor where it came to rest on the toe of her brown Oxford—print side up.

Her heart thudded against her breastbone. The front door bell chimed with the first five beats of *The Sound of Music* and the door opened.

"Hello, Martha. It's me, Arnold. I've finished your walk." Boots thumped and a coat hanger rattled. Footsteps moved along the hallway toward her. "Where are you?"

Martha swooped the paper off her shoe as Arnold Gunther stepped through the doorway.

"Are you okay? You're all flushed."

"I'm fine. Just fine." She flipped over the two sheets on her desk and slammed the third paper—also print side down—on top of them. Then she grabbed her angel paperweight and plunked it on top.

"What did you write about? I bet it was a Valentine story. Can I read it?"

"No, no," she said too quickly. "I mean, you wouldn't be interested."

"I'm always interested in what you write. Let's see it." He reached his hand toward the angel.

Martha covered the crystal wings with both hands. "Really, it's boring this month. In fact, I'm going to redo it."

"I keep telling you, you're too modest. Don't be shy. Let me see it." He leaned forward and touched the top paper.

"Arnold Gunther. Remove your hand from that paper this instant." She jerked the desk drawer open and swept the three pages out from under the paperweight and into the drawer. With a slam, she shut it and twisted the tiny brass key waiting in the lock. She took it out and wrapped her fingers around it. "It's just a silly story. A private silly story."

"Will you let me read it someday?"

Martha tightened her grip on the key and her face turned pink.

The next day, she rewrote her story for the February issue. She didn't put on any music and she typed slowly while the three little kittens played with strands of wool at her feet. Arnold was in the back yard, cleaning off her patio as she wrote about the fluff balls getting themselves tangled up with the wool . . . and one red high heeled shoe.

In March, Arnold came in to check her kitchen sink while she continued the saga of the kittens' rambunctious activities—a hilarious tale of how those mischief-makers had crawled into her bed, cavorted all over her paisley comforter, and lay tumbled in a heap, spent from their kittenish exertions.

In April, she and Arnold went to the movies and held hands like teenagers. The kittens had become permanent residents and with their antics offered great opportunities for her writing.

In May, they went to a church social and dance. His tie was gray. After the dance, he came in for tea, but they had two glasses of wine instead and he kissed her on the mouth and slid his hand down the front of her dress.

At a church meeting, the week before next month's bulletin was due, Mabel Hartley—her blue eyes fixed on Martha's new red shoes—nervously asked if there would be another kitten story. "I don't know why, but lately I feel so taken by your little stories."

And only yesterday at Tuesday's Sewing Circle, Amy Vanhoozen had sidled up to her. It was Martha's turn to make tea, and the water had come to the boil when Amy whispered in her ear about how much she and the other ladies enjoyed the Church Bulletin now. "We get such a thrill out of your kittens' adventures. We can hardly wait for the next tale."

She daren't tell the good church ladies, but last night Arnold had unbuttoned her dress all the way and she let him (*helped him*) remove her bra and underpants. As he quickly disrobed himself, Martha shoed the kittens out of the bedroom, closed the door and suggested he leave his tie on . . . just for fun.

> "I often think that a slightly exposed shoulder emerging from a long satin nightgown packs more sex than two naked bodies in bed.
>
> Bette Davis

Something in your eyes
Quiverdance

There's something in your eyes that says I should apologize
But I don't know what for.
Does it matter anymore?
A hurt that lasts that long must be based in something strong
I need reminding
Of those seventeen year-olds who couldn't fit inside the
      mold
For all their pining

Teenage years are quite a haze, I remember painful days
Some effect I could have had, I don't remember being bad
Just not quite good enough, to find your diamond in the
      rough
and keep it shining

It's thirty-five years passed and you're still looking at my ass
and wondering is she in there?
That seventeen year-old with all her dreams of gold
With silver linings

It's fifty pounds amassed and I'm still looking at my ass
And wondering is she in there?
That seventeen year-old learned not to dream in gold
She's redefining

There's something in your eyes that says I should apologize
You must know what for.
That look evens the score
Forgive me this time round, for we are always bound
in this dance that never ends
to come around again,
in five years or in ten
We can be shining.

"The beauty of a woman with
passing years only grows!"

Audrey Hepburn

Zoe and Her Three Lovers
Mary Ann Moore

An earlier version of this story first appeared as *Ordinary Life*, part of *Hot Shorts: A Story Writing Challenge: Erotica without Exploitation*, in *Prairie Fire*, Autumn 1994.

I live in a small apartment in the Annex in Toronto. It was advertised as three rooms because there is an indentation where the living room ends and the kitchen begins. In fact, it is one large room with a bedroom, a bathroom and a parking space for my lovers. I don't own a car.

I regret the owners weren't true to the original in their renovations. I live in a "modern reno" when I'd rather be living in a 200-year old house in Louveciennes. I feel a need for colour lately. I'd like to paint every room, and indentation, a different colour as Anais Nin did. Lacquer red for vehemence. Pale turquoise for reveries. Peach colour for gentleness. Green for repose. Grey for work at the typewriter, or, in my case, the computer.

Anais gave her typewriter to Henry Miller. I took my vintage typewriter to a used typewriter place on King Street and received enough money to pay my phone bill.

Recently, I watched my DVD of *Henry and June* on my own as Rebecca, my literary lover, was at a writers' conference and Shelagh isn't a fan of Henry Miller and Anais Nin. She probably would have enjoyed the sex.

* * *

The woman sitting beside me at the theatre has an annoying sniffing habit. Her fingers are persistently at her nostrils. I wonder if she can smell her lover there. There is another woman beside her and the two of them are slouched together whispering to each other between sniffs. I'm eating my popcorn, the medium size, sucking the buttery substance from my fingers.

* * *

Shelagh and I like to take food to bed. Sometimes it's Camembert and crackers so we end up with crumbs making a prickly surface for a night of lovemaking. On some occasions we drink wine in the bathtub and waft into bed to massage each other with patchouli body oil. When Shelagh stays the night we make love into the wee hours and sleep late. In the morning we eat fruit in bed and drink coffee from beans I grind. I usually wake first and my first treat of the day is to look at her with just a sheet covering her. Her curly brown hair spirals out to the edges of the pillow. I can just see the rise of her breasts and have the urge to begin stroking her but know we both need nourishment before we begin again. Today I opt for a light kiss on her forehead just at her hairline. I go to the kitchen and get the coffee beans from the freezer. Inhaling their aroma in the grinder, I cringe as I press the top and hope I haven't startled her awake. I get out a basket and put an orange, a banana, a kiwi and a knife in it.

When I get back to the bedroom, Shelagh is sitting up in bed tying back her hair with a rose-coloured ribbon. She's wearing the creamy lace camisole I eased off her body last night. If I could only look at one scene out one window for the rest of my days, let it be this one of Shelagh, her arms reaching up, a smile of welcome on her morning face, thin fabric covering her vulnerability and sensitivity. Let me be the protector, the only one besides herself, to hold the ripened fruit hanging heavy from the bough. I carry the tray to the bedside table and as I put it down she extends a slender arm to grab me and pull me to the bed.

"You smell like a flower in the morning," I tell Shelagh in one of those ears I ran my tongue around in last night.

Shelagh takes the orange and bites into it to break the skin. The torn pieces of bright orange peel go back in the basket. When she's finished, she splits the orange in two, releasing a spray of juice that makes her smile. She tears off a section and puts it slowly in my mouth. Later when I suck her fingers they're covered with a rough substance that's the texture of her own juice.

I met Shelagh when I went to Lichtman's to ask for a back copy of *Yellow Silk*, the journal of erotica published in California. She was standing behind the counter, her hair tied back that day, wearing a white shirt and looking as if she just got out of bed. I told her later she had that just-fucked look—she always does.

"Do you carry back issues of *Yellow Silk*?" I asked her, trying to sound less lascivious than I felt. I had heard that the journal of erotic arts was now selling back issues from the nineties.

"We do but we just get two copies and . . . I buy one of them."

I laughed and said, "Maybe I could borrow yours?"

She smiled back. "Well, it's pretty dog-eared and stained."

I could only imagine what it was stained with. I smiled and she continued:

"Sure, I'll bring it in for you."

"Thanks. I'm thinking of writing some erotica."

"Oh, you're a writer?"

That gets them every time.

* * *

I decide to go to the Bloor Supersave to stock up on Camembert and oranges. The woman is at the corner of Bloor and Madison with her basket. She looks amazingly calm. I try to catch her eye but she looks past me. When I put money in her basket, she looks at me.

"Thank you very much," she says a bit too warmly.

Today the Elvis impersonator has moved to the corner by the Supersave. His cassette player blasts *Return to Sender* while he stands with his legs apart holding his fake microphone. He doesn't move his lips much but I suppose Elvis didn't either. His hair is shiny shoe polish black. His clothes are impeccable. Where did he get those jeans? Today his jacket is a gold fake suede.

I spot Rebecca across the street. Small and serious. She's probably been at Book City.

"Beck, over here." I wave frantically.

She doesn't know where the sound is coming from at first.

Rebecca is intense, a Scorpio. I picked up on that energy as soon as I met her. Very sexual in a smouldering sense not the spiritual way that Shelagh is. Rebecca is a labyrinth of pockets of her past selves that I just can't penetrate. I sometimes get glimpses but that's all she shares. She's dynamite in bed and reads erotica to me over the phone but then she distances herself and when we next meet we start the process all over again. The fact that she's very closeted means I don't run into her at the clubs. I'm encouraging her to do more in the lesbian community. It has given me a sense of solidarity. I know it would do the same for her. I mean, look at Libby. Not that I see her much but sometimes between sit-ins and demos we grab something to eat at the Chinese bakery on Baldwin Street and I get politicized while munching on a pork bun.

Rebecca reads in parking lots. If she's near the end of a book she finishes it, forgetting appointments, arriving with the glazed look of someone who is still on page 276. She's an academic. I dropped out of school to write my first play and didn't go back. I've come to the realization that we have inner resources to tap into and that English courses aren't going to help me write.

I cross the street to meet her.

"Where are you off to?" I ask.

"I'm being interviewed by the CBC. Something about small literary journals. What about you? What are you working on?"

"A new play about the sculptors Frances Loring and Florence Wyle."

"Zoe, what a wonderful idea. I'm amazed no one's done it. But you're just the one. There's a film you know. Made in the sixties. And a book by Elspeth Cameron."

"Yes, I'm reading it." I'm excited by Rebecca's enthusiasm.

"I don't know if we could use the church on Glenrose where they lived but if not, the Haliconian Club, would be a good venue."

"Perfect. Well good luck with it. I can't wait to see it. I really have to go."

"Why don't you come over when you're finished. I'll make you an omelette."

"Okay great. I'll see you."

Another hug and she's gone.

* * *

Rebecca asked me what I wanted. What were my options I wondered. I said, all you've got. I want to make love to you, she said. I want to hear you. I want to run my hands through your hair and have you put your tongue in my mouth. I want to put my breasts against yours. I want to have you hold my head between your legs so I can taste you. I want to hold you from behind and put my hands on your breasts.

I like being made love to from behind, I said.

Where do you want my hands?

I want one hand on the outside on my clit and one inside me.

Jesus. She kept saying Jesus.

* * *

I wrote a story about Shelagh called *Eating in Bed* and sent it to a Women's Press anthology. I've used a pseudonym "Anna Belle" so Libby and Rebecca won't know. If it's accepted and I'm asked to read at the launch, that's another matter. I can always decline but what a great way to meet women. Of course they could fear being included in a short story and having their most intimate secrets known. Shelagh needn't worry. The most revealing bit I wrote about her was that she holds her breath when she comes.

* * *

I was having a shower alone in the cabin with showers and toilets. I heard the outer door open and bang shut. Whoever it was began taking off her clothes near the bench in the outer room where the sinks were. She approached my stall. I could see her though the opaque yellow curtain—brown hair, my height. Dark nipples. Dark triangle. She pushed the shower curtain aside and stepped in. It was Libby. Can I come in she said with a grin. No definitely not. She put her arms around me. Libby don't do this for God's sake. She was kissing my eyelids. The water was streaming down and we were under a waterfall with the smell of forest in our nostrils. She kissed my neck and pushed her breasts against mine. I was dying to caress her breasts. I kept my arms at my sides. Zoe you're beautiful. Oh don't Libby. Please. You know you want me to. But Gayle . . . Gayle is my friend Libby. Please. I want you. She ran her hands through my hair. I put my arms around her neck. She kissed me with her tongue exploring every part of my mouth. She ran her hands down my sides to my waist and then up to my breasts. She played gently with my nipples. Oh God Libby, why are you doing this? Because I've wanted you. You're incredible Zoe. She ducked down to suck on my nipples. I moaned. How could I stop? I tried picturing Gayle walking in. She went further down kissing my belly and then parted my labia to lick my swollen, throbbing clit. She slid one finger in my quim slowly back and forth. I grabbed the top of the stall with my hands. I came with a groan. I wanted her so badly. I tasted myself on her lips and caressed her breasts and put my fingers in her wet cunnis. Fuck me Zoe she said hoarsely into my ear. I hardly moved my fingers. She did it. Rocking back and forth. I kept kissing her so she wouldn't get too loud.

Of course Gayle found out. I said I was sorry. I didn't mean to hurt her. I blamed it on Libby. The middle class was blamed for fostering the ability to do anything, anytime, to any one we damn well pleased.

* * *

It's been two weeks since I talked to Rebecca and as I made a salad for lunch today, I realized it wasn't really her that I miss. It's the parts of me that aren't explored or expressed when I'm not with her.

With Rebecca I really wondered about relationships. How they worked and didn't work. Do I want one? How do I have sex on demand? How do I have sex without daily contact?

I miss Rebecca's sexual energy and the feelings I had with her. She would run her eyes over my body and that's all she had to do to make my nipples hard and my pants wet. Thanking of it now give me flutters in my womb. With her I was not the aggressor; I was the femme. Or I was the expectant child wondering what kind of mood mother is in and what I could do to make things better.

* * *

I ran into Shelagh. I had been exploring the old stomping ground of Loring and Whyle near St Clair and she was leaving

Lichtman's. She was wearing a white peasant blouse off the shoulders and I turned into Clark Gable. I don't play the submissive role with Shelagh. I don't wait for someone else to call the shots or to control me by doling out the affection when they feel able to.

I don't see Libby at all. Libby doesn't make dates and I can understand that she doesn't know how she'll feel on a particular day so she calls me spontaneously. Of course everyone knows I work from home so they always challenge me by asking me out at times when I should be working. If I go out during the day I try to work later but it doesn't always work despite my good intentions.

* * *

I'm left to rejoice in my own body. I suck on my own fingers as I sucked on hers. I feel my own breasts lift them squeeze my nipples run my palms down my belly and gasp at the touch of my swollen clit slide a finger into my opening and heave myself up and down teasing myself with memories of teasing her.

ASPARAGUS

Asparagus is a lovely veg
Its shape could be suggestive
It seems it holds more secrets
Than being just digestive.

According to an herbalist
It stirs up lust in folk.
Bridegrooms should eat three courses
Before that fateful poke

It boosts histamine production
But more importantly than that
It helps produce orgasms
That will surely raise your hat!

The Well
Angelica Sims

She had come to the center of the village, just as she had every day for the last 40 years, to fetch water. He was traveling with a caravan, a group of merchants that had stopped in the desert to camp for the night.

It was here at the well that she encountered this foreigner filling numerous clay vessels and harnessing them onto the back of a sturdy camel. As he lifted the massive pots and secured them with a thick cord, his arms flexed and his torso rippled. She was captivated by his strength. Traces of perspiration beaded on his perfect forehead and broad back.

She was sure he did not come from this part of the world. His dress was entirely different. The leather skirt and helmet indicated he was a Roman soldier and except for the straps that carried a few weapons, his chest was completely bare. Zara had never before seen a man so exposed, especially in the desert sun where it was customary to cover oneself entirely, both out of modesty and as protection from the heat.

She observed him with fascination. At one point he turned to her and smiled. She blushed but could not take her curious gaze away from his captivating presence. A tinge of excitement ran through her and she shuddered. He was the most exotic man she had ever encountered and there was something sensual and seductive in his smile. When his nostrils widened, she breathed deeply too–hoping to inhale even a bit of his scent. While observing the brute strength and unusual features of this man, she began to feel a wonderful sensation rising in her body— something that felt like pleasure.

This foreigner's captivating presence allowed her to fantasize, offering an escape from the reality of her situation. It was over thirty years ago that a tragic and fatal accident ripped her beloved husband from her life. Their children, whom she raised on her own, were now grown and had left home. Life had become barren and cold and it seemed an eternity since she'd known the touch, comfort and warmth of a man beside her. The prospect of being so utterly alone for the rest of her life was an almost unbearable thought, yet a widow was expected to do just this – remain clothed in black and live in celibacy to the end of her days.

Zara had only one jug to fill and he had many. He looked up and drew near, claiming the pot from her hands. She was not certain what to expect, however, he simply filled it and returned it to her with a nod. He was gracious.

She took her pot, realizing that her enjoyment had now come to an end, for how could she sit and admire him any longer? With her task complete, she had no reason to linger. Confused, Zara began down the pathway toward home. She turned back to glance at him more than once, noticing that he too returned her glances. Their encounter was all too brief. Something more needed to be shared between them. But what?

That night Zara could think of nothing but the exotic foreigner and his bronze face. He had green eyes, light wavy brown hair, a chiseled nose and forehead. His appearance was so unlike the other men in the dessert. She dreamed of meeting him again. But what if he was gone tomorrow? What if she were never to see him again? She remained hostage with her own thoughts and was left with rising sexual tension, and longing. Feelings that had seemed forever dormant were now resurfacing in Zara. Engaging with any man was forbidden and the shame, danger and guilt that it involved were unthinkable. Besides, she was certain he was much younger, by at least 20 years, so what could he possibly see in her?

She tossed and turned in bed. The thought of him made her breath quicken and she began to caress herself, first touching her breasts then reaching between her legs to answer to the pulsing and tingling that was present there. She opened herself up and found her body moist and fluid. How long had it been since she had felt such sensations of pleasure? Surprised by her wetness, it invited her to touch every crevasse she could find. Her fever was building and Zara could no longer stay in bed. She rushed outside into the cool night air to refresh herself.

Once outside, Zara stood with her back against the familiar old fig tree, the one she rocked her children beneath when they were babies. The moon was full and there was a slight breeze. What was going on? How could this strange man have evoked such lust in her?

She needed to find him. Zara began to walk toward the encampment where the travelers had pitched their tents that afternoon, just outside the village walls. This was a frightening and risky thing to do. Never had she ventured out beyond the village walls at night without an escort. If anyone were to find her missing, she would be severely punished. And yet, she could not stop herself.

In the distance she could see the faint outline of tents. The full moon guided her along the dirt pathway and through the olive grove. As she drew closer she heard men's voices. Immediately, second thoughts arose. "Maybe this is not such a good idea. What am I doing?" she questioned herself. "There are so many tents, how will I know which is his? And even if I do find him, then what?"

Before she could think any further, she heard heavy footsteps approaching and saw the dark shadows of two fierce men towering over her. Suddenly, she felt a severe and sharp blow to her face and Zara was knocked to the ground. The two thugs grabbed her and covered her head in a dirty burlap sac. There was little air to breath. Her hands were tied tightly behind her back with a rough rope and she was pushed along to an unknown destination. Her pleas for help went unheeded.

She was thrown to the ground and into an empty tent where she lay for a long time. Her heart raced; her mouth was parched and dry. Panic and fear gripped every cell as she gasped for each breath. Over and over she berated herself for such foolish behavior. What would become of her? Would she ever see her family again? It was impossible to tell just how long it had been before the men approached again. They grabbed her a second time and dragged her to another location. There she was made to get on her knees. Finally, the hood was removed from her head and when she looked up, she was eye to eye with the very man she had met that day at the well.

The guards departed and she remained alone with him in his tent. His look and tone were severe and suspect. She had been presented to him as a thief and a spy, and her fate rested in his hands. Zara now knew the full extent of the danger she was in and just how foolish her actions had been. And yet she could not contain her happiness in seeing him again.

"Who are you and what do you want?" he demanded, not seeming to recognize her.

Zara could barely speak. She had to think quickly. "Today, at the well, you filled my water jug. I came only to thank you."

He drew closer then took her face into his hands. He touched the skin where she had received the blow to her face. It was still painful and she winced. He took his time examining her every inch. "I believe you speak the truth," he said. "But there was no need for you to come here to thank me. Where is your home?"

Zara was not sure if it was compassion or anger in his eyes, but she was sure of one thing—these were the same emerald eyes that had captivated her that morning. It was hard for her to answer his question and she didn't. "Your eyes," she said. "They are most beautiful."

At first he seemed irritated by her comment, and then he laughed, as if suddenly realizing just why she was kneeling there in front of him. The tense air between them lifted and he moved to untie her wrists.

"Your family will be worried about you. I will get my horse and take you home."

She felt a fool. Why had she put herself in such an awkward situation? What had she been thinking except of seeing him again? And what horrible things must he be thinking about her?

Together they mounted the Arabian and began riding in

the cool desert night. He placed her in front of him wrapping one arm snugly around her waist while holding the reigns in his other hand. His massive chest moved up and down rubbing her back with every stride and his scent mingled with that of the horse. Having him this close was intoxicating. Zara reached for his hand and guided it inside her warm gown to place it directly onto her soft, bare breast. At that moment, the horse came to an abrupt stop.

He did not remove his hand but advanced it further into her dress rubbing her soft nipple until it rose hard. His head rested on her shoulder and he nibbled at her neck. She turned her head, straining to look at him but could see only the faint outline of his full lips and carved cheekbones. With both hands, he quickly lifted her and turned her to face him then lowered her garment off her shoulders and sunk his head to feast fully on each of her ripe breasts. A new sensation swept over her and she let out a gentle moan. How could a man so rugged as this melt her in such a soft and delicate way? His hands were rough, like the chaff of wheat, yet they touched her like honey.

His mouth was now seeking hers and with an eager tongue he descended upon her lips. She moaned even louder and knew now, deep inside, that it had been her untamed desired for this mysterious man that lead her to venture outside the village walls to risk everything. That warm, now familiar sensation and her silky wetness signaled that it was time to trust him.

In an instant the Roman pulled her off his horse and they both fell to the earth, dizzy with expectancy. He took her hand and led it to the powerful muscle that strained between his legs. Her heart raced with anticipation. Her instincts and the memory of what to do came flooding back as if time had never left its mark. He clasped his hand around hers and lead her in the stroking.

He too was wet with the same clear liquid that was flowing inside her. Her hand slid along his hard, pulsing root. Zara wanted to see his magnificence but the night was too dark. She could only imagine the power of what she was caressing and touching. He seemed to fall weak with pleasure and began to utter incomprehensible words. He then took her face as if he desperately wanted something.

"May I discover you?" he asked. His voice trailed off as he lifted her dress and planted his wanting tongue into her soft, aching center. He swirled inside of her in many directions and she screamed and writhed in pleasure. Her sounds became deep and throaty. With one hand he reached to cover her mouth and with the other he inserted a finger deep inside of her. She jumped at the sensation.

He continued to pleasure her until Zara's excitement could be contained no more. She exploded in a climax that left her breathless, writhing in orgasm and calling out to Allah in praise. When settled, she found him still erect and straining for his own fulfillment. And so, Zara did the most daring of acts, granting him permission to enter her fully into those vast regions that had remained forbidden and untouched for far too long.

They could see the glint in each other's eyes and their lovemaking sent each of them far beyond, into a vast new world. Their bodies were the treasure maps that lead to a temple of ecstasy. When their breathing came to a restful place they peered back at one another from the doorway of their new found universe.

She lay limp, and tucked herself into the safety of his protective arms. His radiant emerald eyes were now well lit by the full moon. Her fingers could not resist combing through his tangled hair. She traced an outline across his broad shoulders, eventually letting her hand come to rest on his heart. "Where am I?" she asked, needing an explanation for this incredible journey.

"We went to heaven," he told her. "Isn't that what you were looking for?"

"Then you and I must be angels," she answered.

"Some say we are Gods."

The rest of the night they danced in the moonlight and entered heaven from many doors. He showed her new ways of pleasuring him. As the light of dawn first approached and without anyone seeing a trace, he lifted Zara once again onto the Arabian and delivered her safely to her home. For Zara there would be no rest.

She learned that his name was Demetrius and that he would be leaving with the caravan the next morning. In a week's time he would return along the same passage. Before he departed they planned their reunion—to meet in heaven again and again, as much as humanly possible.

Ode to a Perfect Pear
Judy Caslor Zarowny

Skin translucent flesh so sleek,
the palest blush upon thy cheek.
I seek thy company and grace
just to view thy perfect face.
Thy miracle of undulation
stirs my heart with expectation,
sears my soul with longing deep
cools my touch, I cannot sleep.
I long to hold thee to my lips
to sink my teeth into thy hips
to rend thy flesh with wild desire
and quench my thirst, put out the fire.

How can I dare this shrine defile
to gratify my senses vile.
Recoil in horror at my lust,
I hang my head in mute disgust.

Tomorrow though, thy flesh will spoil.
The counter top thy hips will soil.
Fair skin will fade to ugly bruise,
wither up and pinkness lose.
And so with tear upon my cheek
I kiss thy face, dig in my teeth.
The sting of sweetness fills the air
Oh thank you dear, dear perfect pear.

FUN SUPPLIES

In your cupboard of armour supplies
Let's not ignore the kitchen.
Very ordinary things
Could be downright bewitchen.

A can of whipped cream in the fridge
Kept cool and at the ready
Can liven up so many things
When she takes off her teddy.

Pile it high and swirl it round,
Put a cherry on the top.
Add a stream of butterscotch,
For a Sunday you'd never swap.

Sprinkle nuts if you've a mind,
To add a little crunch.
Cashews, pecans, hazelnuts,
For you to slowly munch.

And when dessert is over,
Think of all the fun,
When you share a cleansing shower,
Then air dry in the sun.

Lie With Me
Emilia Wildfield

I woke with a start but lay still, waiting for my quickened breathing to slow, the hairs on my arms to settle. Crisp new celadon-colored cotton sheets rough against naked legs. I fell asleep while reading. Draped over my shoulders a shawl clung like a needy boyfriend. The down-filled comforter, wound around my torso, trapped me inside its cocoon. A hint of lavender linen spray, aroused by perspiration, lingered in the creases of my pillow case. Except for Colin's steady breathing beside me, the bedroom was silent.

In my dream, Dan and I were arguing as we walked down a long narrow dimly lit hallway. Every inch of wall covered with paintings in the Dutch style, from a time when merchants demonstrated their accomplishments by having portraits painted. Simple dignified poses captured the Puritan mood. Daunting faces hung so near one another, they might have been standing shoulder to shoulder. Their eyes watched when I leaned close to Dan. His skin smelled of fresh cedar, single malt Scotch and cigars.

"If there's one thing a person should expect from someone who loves him, it is honesty." In my dream, Dan repeated the words from a recent conversation.

"Interesting that you should mention the truth as it looks like I didn't get much of it over X-mas," Dan said last time we spoke. "Just before she flew back to the south of Spain, Melissa announced we were finished."

It must have been lousy for Dan to learn that Melissa was leaving him for good. Even though they didn't live together, even though they didn't live in the same city, a long-distance relationship at its best, they'd been partners for fifteen years.

"This was after a great holiday together," he said. "But she lied to me right through the Christmas holidays. Every time she looked me in the eyes and whispered *I love you*."

In my dream, I'd been trying to convince Dan we should become lovers. But the word *husband* stood in his way.

My husband set the parameters of our marriage long ago. A quick glance at the arsenal of drugs in his medicine chest revealed his fondness for pills. But Colin's conviction that pills could cure just about anything stopped short of swallowing the little blue ones he called *VIGARO*. His personal pharmacy ensured his isolation. Colin never really liked sex, and now he was way past his expiry date in the bedroom. Not that our friends would be convinced about that. Knowing he'd never been faithful distorted their point of view. But Colin's infidelity had little to do with sex. When Colin met Sharon for drinks or a nice dinner, she feigned interest in his stories about corporate takeovers. In return, he flattered her. Egos were stroked more often than sexual organs. Sharon's mother must have told her the same thing mine taught me. A woman knew more about her own body than most men ever would. I tolerated their affair. And somewhere along the way, I learned to appreciate the particular ease associated with a loveless marriage to a rich and powerful man.

But this yearning for Dan introduced a new complication. It forced me to admit I was not free. My husband had abandoned me long ago. And, for the first time, I faced real loneliness.

According to Dan, news that his relationship with Melissa was over came without warning. Everything appeared to be going well. That was obvious when we met at Jen's for a New Year's Day lunch. I greeted Dan with a kiss. And later, my back against the country kitchen pine cabinet, inched over until I leaned against him. Using my index finger to outline the design encrypted around his chest pocket, I complimented him on his new shirt. His reaction was reserved. Other than say it was a gift, he barely responded. Focusing on Melissa, Dan talked about the private party they'd had the night before. A passion-filled celebration shared by the two of them; clothing optional. They both looked happy. He stood tall and said he'd taken his *Cialis* like a good boy. He boasted she was pleased with his performance. *Cialis,* it sounded like a suggestion to *See Alice.* Lucky girl; I wished my name was Alice.

I'd danced with Dan at a party a couple of weeks before that. He took my arm and said, "If you don't mind Amy, this time I'm going to lead." He pulled me closer. "You've been dancing with the same partner far too long. It's time you let someone do something about that." He was just flirting. But it was the most romantic thing anyone had told me for a long time.

Before lunch was served on New Year's Day, Melissa stood near the crackling fire in the living room filled with the smell of burning cherry wood. She wore a white silk blouse and a long purple and grey tartan skirt, the purple the color of amethyst, the grey the color of charcoal, the reflection of flames flickering across the shiny satin. Her skirt hiked in a jaunty fashion on one side showed off new leather boots bought on a recent trip to Paris. She talked about Ramon, the boy in the south of Spain who did chores for her. When asked, she insisted she did not have sex with Ramon. Said she had Dan for sex.

"But what do you do for sex when Dan is not around?" Jen could always be counted on to perk up a conversation. The perfect hostess, Jen was passing around a plate of stuffed potato skins. Ignoring the calorie-rich appetizers, long-married women dressed in outfits of crushed burgundy velvet and moss-colored wool drew closer to Melissa. Drawn like moths to a flame, they longed for something unknown in her answer.

"I masturbate." Melissa held her right hand at an odd angel in front of her, as if to provide proof. "But not as much as I used to."

"You should use a vibrator," Jen said.

"I'm afraid I'd like it too much," Melissa said. "If I got used to it, I'd expect the same pleasure from a man. And that would interfere with our sex."

"You can use it when you're having sex with a man," Jen said.

"Yes." My heart was pounding. "You look up with a smile on your face and say, 'feel free to join in at any time.'"

The women laughed. But it was a vivid picture of ecstasy that made my face flush.

When Melissa and Dan stood next to each other, the sexual attraction was palpable. During last summer's heat wave, it was impossible for a dozen industrial fans blowing full blast to cool the community hall where Jen's art was being exhibited. Rather than glasses of wine, Melissa, Dan and I clutched plastic bottles of ice cold water. While we chatted, moisture beads formed on our bottles. They clung for an instant and then began to trickle down. Dan pressed his dripping bottle against his forehead and said, "Hot." He rolled it against his cheek, neck and exposed chest, each time repeating the word, "Hot." Melissa and I mimicked him. We giggled and hissed until our conversation took on the steamy intensity of a threesome. Hot. Hot. Hot.

News their relationship was over made me realize I'd always been attracted to him. We first met at a one of Jen's dinner parties. When he sat beside me, he commented on the beauty of her elaborate table centre. My eyes grazed the decoration and then focused on him. He was handsome. His voice resonated with the deep muscular tones of someone who sang bass notes. He worked in the film industry which I found exotic. His graying dark hair, neatly tied into a pony tail at the nape of his neck, added to his allure. If pressed, I would have confessed that the flinch in my chest had nothing to do with the number of candles entwined among the fresh arbors which ran down the centre of Jen's antique harvest table. I tried to regulate my breathing. And hoped to appear less interested in seeking his attention than the woman sitting on his other side who announced she had solved the problem of unsightly panty lines, by not wearing underwear.

The wine flowed that evening. Some time after the fresh garlic soup and the New Zealand lamb served with asparagus from Mexico, a platter of nuts and figs and cheeses was passed around. Dan plucked a ripe fig from the plate. He kept it for a moment in his right palm as if weighing its potential. He held it between his long thick forefingers and thumbs, and then split the flesh wide open. He inhaled its perfume, caressed its soft rose and tan fruit, and paused before he scooped out the pulp with his tongue. He smiled, said it was delicious and suggested I try one. My mouth became as moist as an eager bride on her wedding night. Aware of the acute longing between my legs, I swallowed hard.

I'd always ignored those feelings. But too restless to get back to sleep now, I thought about the way Dan crept into my dream. Dream dictionaries say dreams with portraits forecast deception, warn that pleasure will be illusive. And no matter how attractive he found me, despite my interest in him, Dan wanted to be free of deception. Refusing to get involved with anyone who could not commit full-time, he turned me down.

To show their success, rich merchants commissioned portraits of their wives. Unremarkable women dressed in black, row upon row of resigned faces bordered by broad white ruffs. I studied these forlorn women enclosed in frames, each of them as untouchable as a still life. And I recognized them. They were portraits of me.

The Plumber
Wendy Simmons

I snuggled under my flannel sheets in my comfy bed as I finished the last page of *50 Shades of Grey* and I admit that my glasses were almost steamed up. Nothing like those things in the book had ever happened to me. Then again, I don't think I would want handcuffs or whips. Or would I? Maybe a little. Maybe gently.

My mind wandered to something that had happened two days ago. The cold water pipes under the kitchen sink had frozen up and I had to call a plumber. My usual guy was out sick so I called a company I had never used before. When I opened the door to the new guy I inwardly gasped. At least I hope he didn't hear me. Talk about hot! What is it about a tool belt that looks so darned sexy anyway? Just a bunch of long hard steel tools hanging around a slim waist, pulling the jeans down ever so slightly. Okay, I think I get it. It certainly had an affect on me.

I stood there staring stupidly at this young, juicy, red blooded, oh so good looking male in my doorway.

"You called a plumber, Ma'am?"

Oh my god, he called me Ma'am. He thinks I'm ancient and here I am drinking him in like hot rum.

"Yes, I'm sorry. Come on in. My kitchen pipes are frozen and I'm afraid they're going to burst." *That's not all that's going to burst!*

I opened the door wide and led him to the bedroom. I mean kitchen. *Damn, he is so freaking sexy.*

"So when did you first notice they were frozen?" he asked in a voice that wrapped around me like melted chocolate.

"Last night but I didn't want to call anyone out that late. I figured it would be okay to wait until morning."

"Don't worry about calling late. I'll come whenever you need me."

Really? Define "need." I must keep that in mind. In fact, define "come." Stop it!

I hope the pipes haven't split from being frozen so long. Let's have a look"

With that he opened the cupboard and hunched down for a better look.

God, look at those broad shoulders and that narrow waist. And his T-shirt is riding up and the jeans snugging down just a tad more. Mmmmmm. Wait, was he saying something? "I'm sorry, what was it you said?"

"I said it looks as if I'll be able to warm up the pipes with my blow torch and that should fix it."

*Did he just say **blow** torch? How did he mean that? Is he sending me a message? Damn, I wish my body would let my brain work.*

I felt a blush creeping up my face so turned away and grabbed a dish towel. As it happened there were no dishes to dry so I landed up wringing my hands in the stupid towel, feeling like an idiot. What am I, seventeen? Unfortunately, nowhere near. Three times that in fact. No wonder he called me ma'am. "Great"

I replied lamely.

Next thing I know he's laying on the floor, stretched out in all his hunkedness with his arms under my sink. *That T-shirt is riding up even higher as he reaches for the pipes. Could he get any hotter?* I did have to ask, didn't I?

I feel as if I am in the middle of an X-rated movie! No wonder they always use hot guys with tool belts. Is someone filming this?

All of a sudden there's a whoosh and water streamed out from under the sink straight at him. He jumped and reached for the turnoff valve but not before I was witnessing a wet T-shirt contest in my kitchen. I was standing close enough that my pant legs got wet as well. He scrambled up and we stood there laughing awkwardly as he stripped off his shirt and there, in all its glory, was the "any hotter" that I had been thinking about. I saw a movie once where a young woman was looking at a guy who had taken off his shirt. She made some comment about him having been photo-shopped. That comment would have fit this guy's body perfectly. I once more drank in that hot rum and this time it went straight to my knees.

What on earth?

"Excuse me, I have to go and take my pants off," I stammered.

Sweet baby Jesus, did I really say that?

He lifted an eyebrow. "Go for it. Then we'll both be half naked."

Was that a sly grin I just saw?

"Need any help?"

This can't be happening. Not to me. He must have meant

something else.

"Thanks, but I think I can manage," I mumbled and headed toward the bedroom.

By the time I got back he had fixed the leaking pipe and had my water running again. *No kidding!* With my dry jeans on and firmly zipped up, I had managed to cool off somewhat and come to my senses. He was gathering his tools and jamming them back into his belt slowly, one at a time. With each thrust his pants seemed to be dipping a little further down, or was it just because he didn't have a shirt on? *Go further! Go further!*

"I'd offer you a shirt but there isn't a man of the house and I don't think you would fit into any of mine."

But I'm sure there is something of mine he could fit into. Oh no. Here I go again.

These wanton thoughts led to a certain dampness that would soon be telling on my snug fitting jeans. What on earth was happening?

Nature. Sex appeal. Hormones. Lust. Need. Now . . .

"Thanks all the same but I always carry a couple of shirts with me. This isn't the first time I have been soaked on the job. Anything else I can do for you before I leave?"

Soaked. Wet. Sliding. YES!

"I think all my other pipes are working well, thanks.

I have turned into a raving idiot! Come on brain, say something intelligent. Maybe he really is interested in doing more than working on your plumbing.

Do you have a card in case I need you again?" I asked.

He pulled a card out of those tight jeans and stepped toward me to hand it off. Was he leaning just a little closer than necessary? His hand brushed mine as he gave it to me and he looked straight into my eyes.

"Call me any time. I'm a man of many talents."

I glanced at the card and saw that he also worked on Air Conditioners. That must be what he meant.

I saw him to the door. He took a step out and then turned to me and said, "Call me. I'm sure there is something I can do for you. Anytime."

And with that he left.

By this time I was almost gushing as much as my burst pipes. I ran to the kitchen, flew open the cupboard doors where he so recently had been lying, and tended to my screaming body right then, right there. Thank God I am an accomplished do-it-yourselfer. I looked out the kitchen window over the sink just in time to see my Adonis wave to me from his truck at the very moment my personal pipes burst with an audible grown that I was sure he could hear over his truck engine.

And here I was, two days later, laying in bed thinking what an idiot I had been. Why not take a chance? He had certainly acted as if he wanted to do more than just my plumbing and I was certainly willing for him to *do* my anything, anytime. I should call him. But what could I say? I can't make my pipes freeze again. Hell, I could hit them with a sledge hammer and wouldn't hesitate if it got him back here. I could drop something down the drain and need him to retrieve it. That wouldn't take very long to fix and we would have time for any other jobs I might want him for. Yes, I'm going to do it.

OMG, here I go again. Doing it yourself is one thing but I really would love the real thing once in a while. How long has it been? Too long.

The next morning, I carefully dropped my ring down the drain. Not an expensive one, just in case he couldn't get it back, but a nice enough one to be a good excuse. I grabbed his card and dialed as I walked into my bedroom (might as well visit the scene of his future job) and waited for him to answer.

When his sexy voice on the answering machine finished, I said in a sultry voice, "Hi, this is Jeannie calling from Sycamore Drive. You were here a couple of days ago working on my pipes. I, um, dropped a ring down the kitchen sink and wondered if you could come and get it out for me. I was going to wash the dishes but realized I had it on and while taking it off my slippery hands down it went! It's one of my favourite rings and . . . "

You're babbling! Stop it! "So. Right. I'll be in all day so call me, okay?" I hung up feeling like a flustered teenager again. *Am I really going through with this?*

I puttered around trying to stay calm. *What should I wear? Something easy to get out of, obviously. Should I guide him toward the bedroom? Should we do it on the couch? In the kitchen? Hell, I don't care as long as we do it somewhere!*

An hour later Mr. Toolbelt called. His voice was as delicious as I remembered. He sounded pleased that I had called and said he would come around eleven. He had another job that he needed to finish.

He ended with a smooth, "looking forward to seeing you."

Warmth immediately spread through me as I imagined him coming into the house. This time I was not going to let him escape until we were both thoroughly satisfied that the job was well and truly done.

I fussed around watching the clock while I changed twice. I put on my tightest jeans, sans underpants. The thought of him walking in with me in no undies was getting me more than ready for him. In fact, the seam in my jeans was already doing a great prep job. A flimsy top would fit the bill as well. No bra, of course. Nipples reaching out for him would leave no doubt in his mind as to my expectations. *Who cares. It's time I was a bit of a hussy. I've been too proper all my life and this one time I'm going for it.*

At five to eleven I was more than ready to receive my visitor. I had left a note on the door telling him to come in. Place was tidy, ready to be messed up, and I hoped I looked as hot as I felt. Nerves were jangled and moisture was building in all the right places.

I heard the truck in the drive and just then the phone rang. *To heck with that. Let it go to voicemail. I'm ready for an adventure and don't want to get stuck with some telemarketer or worse yet, my mother.*

I planned on making my grand entrance once he was lying on the floor.

Straddling is fun too.

The door opened and closed and I held back a scream of raging lust. I waited a couple of moments until I heard those long hard tools jangling into the kitchen. When I felt he must be on the floor, I took a deep breath and sauntered into the kitchen doing my best to look sexy and alluring.

What the @#*?

The man bending down at my sink with his tools was not my Mr. Toolbelt. This one was at least 300 pounds and balding.

The T-shirt that stretched over several bulges revealed love handles that I wouldn't be able to grasp with an extra pair of arms. An ass crack a mile wide that his jeans couldn't cope with, smirked at me.   My libido took a nosedive and my nipples cowered under my blouse in fright. I stood there gaping in disbelief and disappointment.

"Oh, hi," said my nightmare plumber. "Randy couldn't make it so he asked me to drop around. He had a fender bender, but he's okay. He said he was disappointed not to make it and that he was going to call you. Surprised he didn't."

The phone call! I could have saved myself from looking like an ass (or at that ass). Hopefully this guy couldn't tell what I had been expecting. Certainly my cowering nipples didn't give me away.

"Here's the ring. It was so easy to get to I won't even charge you," he chimed, holding forth my planted jewellery.

"Ah, ya, thanks," I stammered as he packed up and headed for the door.

So much for my morning tryst with the Mr. Toolbelt.

As the truck crunched out of the driveway, I headed for the phone.

Hmmm, I really need an air conditioning estimate. Hell, I'm going to call him and tell him to get himself over here. One very good reason, no excuses.

Answering machine again. "Hi Randy, give me a call when you can. I still need your experienced touch on some things. Hope to see you soon."

OMG what have I done? Am I nuts? No! Bring it on . . .

Impertinent
Harry Posner

It is going to be a 'he', that much you know. Has to be a 'he' for any of it to make sense.

At first it announces itself in snatches of memory, floating through the window of your mind during the early hours of the morning: the electric feeling of Tony Spellerini's fingers on your breasts, that Sunday behind the school, the two of you cloistered in a dark doorway. Your hand feeling its way down to the hard lump trying to push its way through his jeans; a grey misted image of you as a young girl straddling Rocket's bare back, tiny shivers of energy fluting up your spine with each galloping stride; Brian's goodbye kiss, the morning you left for the convent, stolen in a lurching moment of desire, the feeling of his warm tongue in your mouth.

Thirty-three years contemplating God in all His glory, wisdom and Love. A Love that arrives in forms too numerous to know, in ways too mysterious to fathom. But Mother Superior has always encouraged the Sisters to develop enquiring minds. It is not enough to be pious, she would say, or to carry a compassionate heart. One has to, as she puts it, become *innocently impertinent in the face of God's mysteries.* A hard one for a good Catholic girl raised in a good Catholic household, whose vocation had made itself known to her in the form of tears leaking from the eyes of her favorite Teddy bear at the age of seven.

Now, after the doctor's beige-toned news—*Sister, the truth of the matter is that we don't know how much time you may have left. It could be weeks or it could be months*—you decide to heed Mother Superior's words.

What comes, comes, not in the form of a question, innocent and impertinent. What comes, comes in the form of a prayer. A strange and private affair. Hands together, gazing up at the Crying Jesus of San Sebastien, as it is known, you remind the Lord of His unending mercy (impertinent), how He gives His Love in ways unfathomable. *Heavenly Father*, you pray, *I don't ask for peace at the end, nor am I afraid of pain. There is only one thing I wish for, Father, one thing neither given nor received in my lifetime.* You hesitate, then plunge on. *Please let him be gentle and kind, and let him want me more than I've ever been wanted before. Let him touch me, Father. Let him touch me to my deepest core. Let him touch me until I cannot stand to breathe. Amen.*

When finally he comes to take you away, your breathing is shallow, eyes half closed. You almost don't recognize him when he arrives, so gradually does he approach. He appears as a slender ripple in the air, moving slowly towards you. The ripple lifts the sheets at the foot of the bed and slips under. In an instant you feel his cool fingers on your skin. Waves lapping at your shore. Deeper. Crashing, pounding. Eyes widen with ecstasy. Until breath forgets to breathe. Until he has fingered and kissed all of the sacred objects wrapped and hidden in your Holy of Holies. The mystery of His Love manifest in the smiling lips of a dead woman.

Something Old Something New
Sholmes

Reluctantly, Emma relinquished her black leather blazer and grabbed the coat check ticket from a very bored, very young man. She had chosen her outfit deliberately because the jacket nicely hid bulges. Had she known she would be forced to give it up she would've worn the waistless shift instead. Already she was annoyed and she hadn't even entered the Legion hall yet. Her irritation was more about finding herself at this place on this night than it was about the jacket, but it felt more sensible to focus on her clothes rather than her presence.

Imagine a woman her age attending a singles dance. It was absurd, laughable even. Only desperately lonely folks would come out for something like this. People would think she was pathetic.

Well, in truth, she was pretty lonely. If she spent one more Friday night watching CSI marathon reruns she would run naked through back yards screaming. Then her neighbours would call the men in white suits to give her a new blazer—one where the sleeves tied in back—and take her away.

Emma chuckled to herself at that bit of melodrama and resolved to at least give the night a chance. She ducked into the ladies, applied fresh lipstick and fluffed her salon blonde curls with her fingers. She sighed at her reflection. When did she get so old? At what point did the years start to leave insidious little traces of their journey on her face? Poking at the bit of belly spilling over her waistband, she bemoaned the beer she had indulged in more often than not.

"Oh well," she said to her mirror image. "This is who you are now and you're here so get on with it girlfriend."

She had barely left the bathroom when Rosalie's shrill voice carried its message over the tiny crowd. "There you are Emma," she trilled "I've been looking everywhere!" Considering the foyer was minuscule and the hall not much bigger, Emma couldn't imagine where her friend had looked but she addressed her warmly just the same.

"Here I am, Rosalie, as promised."

"I'm so glad you came. I had my doubts you know."

Emma did know. She had declined this invitation on several occasions and only agreed this time because the sight of her four apartment walls was driving her to distraction. She needed a diversion, a night away from home and some different scenery. Her hope was to have a conversation or two with someone other than her cat or Rosalie. That wasn't about to happen if she perched on her couch night after night for the rest of her life. Rosalie was outspoken and a bit rough around the edges but she was the best friend Emma had. Her short straight bob was a brilliant burgundy tonight, the hue of her hair matching the over-the-top application of eye shadow. Multiple chains jangled around her neck, falling almost to her waist, doing nothing to draw the eye away from her incredible bulk. That is a big difference between us, Emma thought, I'm always trying to hide myself where Rosalie doesn't care what people think. She envied that.

"Do you have a table?' Emma asked as Rosalie hooked an arm through hers and steered her towards the bar.

"Let's get drinks first and then we'll sit. Okay?"

"Sure," said Emma. She gladly let Rosalie lead the way while she examined her surroundings. The Legion was old and dated but someone had made an effort by painting the wood panelling white and stencilling ivy all around the middle. Massive spring bouquets, spilling over with colour, adorned every table. Strings of tiny white lights quivered and blinked under the push of ceiling fans.

"A couple of beers please." Rosalie's voice boomed through Emma's scrutiny.

She glanced up to find herself at the bar. Gratefully, she accepted the ice cold Coors Light. It gave her something to do with her hands which would hopefully hide her nervousness."So, where we sittin'?"

Rosalie glanced this way and that and dropped her voice to a whisper. "Weeeell,' she spread the word out warily. "We're not actually sitting together."

"What?" Emma cried. Rosalie was the only person she knew there and she was feeling self conscious enough without having to roam the room alone. What could her friend be thinking? "What do you mean we're not sitting together?"

Without realizing it Emma had been manoeuvred clear across the room. They approached a table for four with a lone man sitting at it. As he rose in greeting, Emma had a twist of déjà vu but before she could analyze it, Rosalie was making introductions.

"You remember Jamie Brownlea, don't you Emma?"

Jamie Brownlea! Jamie Brownlea was her high school boyfriend. Jamie Brownlea was the boy she'd loved desperately as only a sixteen year old can. Jamie Brownlea was the **one** to whom she gladly, willingly gave her virginity. Jamie Brownlea had proposed marriage to her.

Jamie thrust out his hand and gripped hers. "You haven't changed a bit, Emma Smart."

Bullshit, thought Emma. The same smooth voice and even smoother lines of flattery. The last person she ever expected to see was Jamie Brownlea. Never had she forgotten the pain of that love—her first. Did he think she didn't remember that he got another girl pregnant, swearing up and down the baby was not his? That he had betrayed her, left her and married another. That he had broken her heart?

She jerked her hand away, red heat rising to her face. Her breathing was erratic. Consciously she slowed it down and fought to regain her composure. Jamie was looking at her curiously. He probably thought she was having a stroke.

"Are you all right, Emma?"

His concern seemed genuine and Emma felt foolish. In the time it took her to find her voice, after those flash frames of thirty year old memories, Rosalie had disappeared.

"Sorry Jamie," she managed with some normalcy. "I'm just surprised to see you. What's it been? Thirty years?"

"Thirty-two," he said with a piercing stare. "And four months and seven weeks."

Emma couldn't respond to that. Her eyes locked with his and briefly the love those eyes had once conveyed to her, sparked again. She promptly blocked the recollection and averted her eyes, searching the room for Rosalie to rescue her. No luck. Jamie clasped her elbow and lowered her into a chair. Not knowing what else to do she settled on the seat. A memory came of a room much like this one, people sitting about in small groups, the veneer tables scarred and the decorations uninspired. It was Coke they drank back then, although they'd been known to sneak in some rum on occasion. But the boy was the same—a lot older now and a little softer around the edges. Back then there was a fizz of excitement in her blood. More than sexual heat, anticipation for the future and all that life would throw at her.

Her thoughts were drawn up short when Jamie pushed himself abruptly into her space. Grabbing the chair next to hers, he slid it even nearer and leaned his face in tight. It was too close for comfort and Emma wrenched herself back against her seat. Apparently he got the message because he sloped back a little as well.

"I suppose it is a shock." He started. "I knew you and Rosalie were friends and I begged her to bring you along some night. I just learned you were here myself." He paused. When she didn't speak, he continued. "I'm so happy to see you, Emma. I've wanted to talk to you for so long."

Afraid her voice might break like a prepubescent boy's, Emma stayed mute but her brain had lots to say. *Talk then you sonofabitch. Explain yourself if you think you can. Better make it quick 'cause I'm outta here.* "So talk," she said out loud. *Shit. She sounded like an eight year old trying on attitude.* Panic snaked its fingers in her belly once again and started to climb. *What could he want to talk about? What would he think of her now? Dammit Emma, you don't care anymore. Right?*

Jamie seemed sincerely baffled by her response, or lack there of. "Are you *still* angry with me Emma?"

"Don't be ridiculous." Again with the attitude. *Chill out Emma. Let the man talk if he must.*

"Emma." Jamie's voice was slow and steady and calm. Gently, he pried her clenched fingers from the beer bottle. As he rubbed her hands in his, the chill from the drink went away. "I've pined for you Em. My whole life."

The DJ had started to spin and music hummed all around them. Eager dancers tapped by, but it seemed as though they were the only two people in the room. Fear paralyzed her. Fear of rejection. Again. She had pined for him too.

At last he broke the awkward silence. "My *whole* life," he repeated.

Astonished, disbelieving, and confused, Emma's eyes betrayed the cold demeanour she had strived to project. A tear slipped from the corner. "Wanna get out of here? Go somewhere and talk?" It was Emma who had finally spoken, the headstrong, inflexible Emma who so far had barely said a word.

"Yes," said Jamie, letting out his breath. "Yes, I do."

* * *

Jamie's house, though old and small, was lovingly cared for and efficiently updated. He steered her towards the butter soft leather couch and went to fetch her a drink. Handing her a beer, he immediately launched into an explanation. He sat at the end of the couch and seemed anxious and hurried, like he wanted to get it all out as quickly as he could.

"The baby I swore was not mine? Well, it was. I was a stupid, horny teenager and Elaine was a willing participant. Our parents forced us to marry with disastrous results and she had a difficult labour resulting in a stillborn boy." He rushed on. "She was inconsolable and swam to the bottom of a vodka bottle. I chose bourbon." He looked at Emma. "The booze helped me forget about you, and forget about the huge mistake that had changed my life. I always regretted the pain I caused you." He didn't wait for her to speak. "It hit me how my behaviour had ruined my own life. There I was—miserable, in a loveless and now childless marriage—and I continued to drink. The more I drank the angrier I became and the angrier I became the more I drank. I was caught in a vicious circle with no end in sight." He stared into the glass in his hand. "I was fired repeatedly from jobs, we lost our house and whatever small connection we might have once had, vanished with it. One night, Elaine stumbled drunkenly into an oncoming tractor-trailer and ended her life." He took a long drink. "I blamed myself and sunk into a deep depression. Booze and pot became my crutches for the next ten years. Friends and family tried to help, but I refused to listen and one by one they all let me go until I was completely alone."

Emma reached out a hand and laid it on the soft cushion between them. "Jamie—"

"No, let me finish. A few years back, wallowing in self-contempt, I took my first tentative step towards healing by seeking a therapist. I got sober, I got perspective and . . ." He looked up at her. "I even went looking for you. But by then you had married and, as selfish as I was, I couldn't bring himself to intrude on that. "I though about you every single day," he'd admitted sheepishly.

They placed their drinks on the coffee table and moved toward each other. The first kiss was tentative and slow. God she hadn't kissed in ages. She felt awkward and silly. Unable to stop herself, she laughed nervously.

"Seems a little surreal, after all these years." He grinned. "Let's try again."

The second attempt outshone her meagre expectations. Passion flared up in her, like a dormant fire that had laid low for much too long. It was as if she had forgotten her body once belonged to a sensual, highly sexual woman. A pleasing ache started in her pelvis which involuntarily rocked her hips. Her apprehension vanished. Suddenly she could hardly wait. When Jamie's hand softly cupped her breast she placed her palm over his and squeezed, making him clench harder. When Jamie's fingers fumbled with her bra strap, she reached back and flipped the clasp. When he lifted her from the couch and carried her, like she weighed no more than a child, to his bed she thought she might die from the need of him. Once on top of his duvet, she hastily began to remove her clothes. Jamie stilled her hands.

"Let me." His voice had a seductive hum. "Please."

Control was essential to Emma and it was difficult to let someone take the lead. Jamie's eyes never left hers as he undid the few remaining buttons of her blouse and removed the dangling bra. He gazed at her breasts.

"These are as delectable as I remember," he panted and softly licked one breast and then the other. The gentleness became stronger and harder until her breathing was jagged and her breasts tender from the manhandling. She didn't give a hoot! Bring it!

He slipped his hands slowly down her torso, awakening every nerve ending. Her pulse quickened as he skimmed over her tummy and gently pulled down her stockings. Lifting his bulk from the bed he continued tugging until her skirt lay in a purple puddle on the floor. He hooked a thumb under her panties and eased them off her hips. The thin lace stroking her legs felt delicious all the way down past her toes. He then shucked off his own shirt and jeans. Emma hungrily eyed his trim body. Jamie was as tall and almost as lean as she remembered him as a teenager. Joining her back on the bed, he laid the full length of his naked body against hers and pulled her close. Heat generated between them. As his arms wrapped around her, their mouths met again. He parted her lips with his tongue and took charge of the kiss. She responded in kind, streaming her hands up and down his body, feeling every inch of him.

He moaned and spoke in a winded murmur. "Oh, Emma, you are as beautiful and sexy as always. I can't wait to have you."

His thumb found her vagina, moist and ready to accept him. "Ahh," she sighed, "I always loved your thumbs."

"I remember," he sniggered and accelerated his pace. Emma felt sixteen again, and as if those thirty odd years had not passed without them being together. She gave herself up to the pleasure of his ministrations and soon gushed out an orgasm that soaked both them and the bed.

"So that hasn't changed either." Jamie smiled and scooted them both over to a dry spot. Emma remembered the humiliation of the first time that happened (and subsequent times with new men over the years). They had been at the lake in his father's car. She thought she had peed and was ashamed. Turned out that's just the way it works for her. But she felt no such embarrassment with Jamie. He was there the very first time and, like now, completely cool.

"My turn," he said. He flipped her over and pulled her to the edge of the bed. "On your knees," he commanded and Emma was happy to comply. He stood behind her, off the bed, and gently, at first, eased his rock hard penis into her slot. Man, that feels good, she thought. Leisurely he dragged his penis out almost all the way and then slowly pushed it back in until he filled her completely. The sluggishness of his pace made her impatient and she wanted to shout at him to go faster.

As if he could read her mind, he smirked. "Have patience little girl. Relax and enjoy." Before she could protest, he sped up his pace. His cock pounded in her all the way and then out to the very tip and then in again what seemed like a hundred times. Each thrust left her gasping for air. Her fingers tugged at the messy duvet cover and sheets. Reaching out blind she found a pillow, grasped it and tucked it under her tummy for support. "Gimme all you got baby," she demanded and he did. Relentlessly he plunged himself in and out of her. Each thrust filled her completely; every lunge touched all sides, the momentum escalated until their rocking made the bed collide with the dresser.

"Oh my god," she squealed as his orgasm exploded within her. Not ready to quit, he slowed his pace, clenched his hands together under her belly, and hoisted her hips upward. He hauled her bum around in circles, his cock still in her. It was heaven, glorious sexual heaven. Finally he stopped and as she crawled forward to lie exhausted on the bed his penis slipped from her. Jamie dropped down beside her, his heart pounding, his breath erratic, and his satisfaction obvious.

For a while they lay there, just catching their breath. Emma had not felt so alive, so sexy, so satiated in many years. If this was it, if this was all they ever again had, she was grateful for it. Jamie was, most definitely, damaged goods, and maybe this was all he could give her now. He snuggled in tight, spooning her naked body with his. He nuzzled the back of her neck, all the while she felt his body trembling.

"I hope someday you can forgive me" He wept, openly and honestly. "For being such a fool."

Emma turned her body around, pressed her breasts against his chest and softly fingered the tears on his cheek. "I just did," she whispered.

This time their lovemaking was more deliberate, less frenzied. Jamie's hands floated down her back, cupped her bum and moved in front to fondle her pussy lips. He spread them apart and gazed at them in awe like he had never seen another. Gingerly he touched his lips there and she moaned with pleasure. He added first one finger and then another, and Emma felt a vibration race from her pelvis down her legs. She shuddered with lust. Just when she thought she could die from the ache of wanting him, Jamie slithered deliciously back up and entered her dripping vagina with ease. They rocked, missionary style, up and down and back and forth forever, every stab feeling better than the one before. Her hips rose to meet him, blow for blow until the driving force propelled them both into a walloping climax.

Jamie was soon asleep, but Emma's brain would not shut off. She revelled in the comfortable feel of a man wrapped around her. Vulnerable in slumber, he had murmured her name twice. It had been a long time since she'd had that. It had been thirty-two years, four months and seven weeks since she'd known real love. Would it even be possible for her and Jamie to have that again? Delicately, she extricated herself from beneath the weight of his arm, pulled his undershirt on over her nakedness and crept from his bedroom.

Helping herself to a glass of milk, she wandered the darkened rooms alone, glimpsing bits of his life in fridge art and proudly displayed photos. Wearing nothing but his T-shirt made her feel very sexy and just a bit embarrassed by the crazy, monkey sex they had just shared. Pleased to have time alone to reflect, she sunk into the butter brown leather couch and piled a fleece throw over her legs. Emma was a thinker. Sometimes it was a blessing and sometimes a curse. With Jamie fast asleep she could relive every moment in her head.

* * *

"I was afraid you'd left."

Startled, Emma emerged from her reverie, a satisfied smile on her face. Jamie sat next to her. From his face, he seemed relieved at finding her there on his couch. For a boy who turned into a liar and a cheat he was now certainly a man unafraid of honesty. Perhaps all those years they spent apart were good. Often she had indulged in the fantasy that they had married when they were supposed to but always the reality of Elaine and the lies intervened. She had convinced herself that it would never have worked. Not then—but maybe now?

"And if I had left?" She teased.

"I would track you down and drag you back into my bed." He laughed.

Emma leapt from the couch and raced down the hall. "Last one there is a rotten egg," she chirped and her heart filled with joy as he rushed up behind her.

"Aging is not lost youth but a new stage of opportunity and strength."

Betty Friedan

Ode to pickles
Quiverdance

my favorite pickle is the dill
it certainly gives me quite a thrill
it's long and firm with a nice tart flavour
the juicy squirt I love to savour
but nothing pickled can quite match
the joy I've tasted from your pickle patch
the long hard shaft no jar could contain
and the ferocious spurt my throat would detain
I can suck dill pickles 'til I'm blue in the face
but none come close to your animal grace
their balls don't tighten nor their head peek through
even adding pickled onions just won't do
my favorite pickle is the dill
but it doesn't give me enough of a thrill
your manhood before me is what I pretend
until I bend over and bite off the end.

The Awakening
Chapter One from the novel
The Late Bloomer: Confessions of a Sex Addict
Sherry Somerville

For my 50th birthday, my friends and colleagues at Industrial Life threw a surprise party for me to start my next decade. It wasn't the only surprise I got that night.

At the end of the evening, I gathered my gifts, and as I was saying my thank you's and good bye's, Tom Richards from Advertising offered to drive me home. Tom was an Aussie who had only been with the company for three weeks. Jeannette, at personnel, had passed the lowdown on him to all the girls in the office. He was 27, single and drove a vintage Austin Healy. We didn't need to be told he was drop-dead good looking, six feet tall and regularly worked out at the gym.

So the other women raised their eyebrows and tittered when I walked out with Mr. Awesome. Little did I realize that the next hour would change my life. That I would be propelled into places and feelings I never dreamed existed. That I would not only find my purpose but a whole new reason and passion for living.

But right now I simply enjoyed having a handsome young man carry my parcels, help me in and out of his low slung vehicle and walk me to the entrance of the Victoria Gardens

Complex where I lived.

"Let me help you to your apartment," he said, his arms full of birthday packages.

"Thank you, Tom. That's very kind of you." Such a nice young fellow.

We didn't speak in the elevator or as we walked along the eleventh floor hallway. I fumbled for my key, opened the door and we entered.

"Just put them there," I said, and pointed to the beige paisley couch.

He tumbled the parcels out of his arms, turned to me and said, "Happy Birthday. See you Monday." He leaned over and brushed a light kiss on my cheek. I must have moved slightly because his lips touched the corner of my mouth. A spark jumped between us.

"Oh my," I said. A tingle skipped through my solar plexus.

"Oh, wow," he said. He put his full lips on my mouth and stayed there. I didn't move away.

His tongue pushed my mouth open and he thrust it deep into me, exploring and probing. My body leapt at him, pressing against him as I met his tongue with mine.

No one had ever kissed me like this. What was happening to me? My body was on fire. I wanted—no needed—this young man to engulf me, and I him.

We tore at our clothing, yanking at buttons, pulling zippers, feverish to touch, to feel, to get at each other. Reason had completely gone from me. I was a wild animal swamped with desire.

With one swift movement, he ripped my underpants open

and his throbbing hardness found my wet entrance and plunged in. We fell on my birthday gifts, shoved them aside, and there amongst ribbons and wrappings, in less than a moment I, Sherry Marie Somerville, with this tremendous young man banging on top of me, experienced the big O for the first time in my life. O with a capital letter. O as in OMG! O as in OOOOHHHH!!!

Yes, I had my first orgasm. So this was what all the fuss was about with sex. My body quivered and shivered and shook. The earth stood still and the heavens exploded in a canopy of fireworks while the 1812 Overture resounded in my head.

I had found my purpose.

This was what life was all about.

After that incredible burst of quantum energy, I collapsed and lay replete and at peace, floating in a bubble of wholeness and plenitude. Filled up. Satiated. Connected to every particle in the Universe. At one with God.

The man named Tom pulled out of me. "What just happened?" he said.

"Life just happened," I murmured as I swooned in delicious ecstasy.

* * *

The Late Bloomer is available as a paperback or e-book
at Amazon.com

OYSTERS

These slimy little buggers
Are ugly as can be
And yet when on the half shell
Go for a hefty fee

Visit any local bar
They'll be on many tables
Men have listened carefully
To the many fables

Is it fiction or is it fact
What these slippery things can do?
Be an aphrodisiac?
Have that effect on you?

So go ahead if you do dare
Eat the little blobs of jelly
They'll make their way to other parts
just below the belly!

The G.T.
Caitlin Smith

It's Saturday afternoon and I am alone in the house. I stroll into the kitchen and make myself a pot of tea. The kids are at work, and then they will go to their dad's house for the rest of the weekend to spend time with him and "the bitch." They call Shelley that; I don't—well, at least I don't call her that out loud. They don't like their stepmother and it's hard for me to blame them. After all, how can you like someone who tore your home apart?

It's particularly difficult for my daughter, Beth. She and Shelley don't agree on much and it hurts her that her father consistently sides with Shelley when she and Beth lock horns. Of course, Beth comes to me, full of anguish and I have to be the mature, calm adult and, while I can't make it seem reasonable that her father should agree with Shelley's madness, I have to try and cool her down and keep her from doing something foolish like posting on Facebook or calling Shelley names or permanently damaging the frail relationship she has with her father. And, however it turns out, I will be in the wrong with Shelley and Ben.

My serenity shattered, I fling the last of my tea into the sink, rinse the cup and try to calm down. I'm always so angry or on edge lately. I used to be able to role with the punches like our son Sam. At twenty-two, he's so much more even keeled and tolerates Shelley better. Besides, he only goes to stay at his dad's house because it's so much closer to Sarah's place and he wants to spend all his time with her.

Sam and I had one of those delicious heart to heart conversations a few weeks ago when he came in late from a date with Sarah and I was on one of my nocturnal wanders through the house. At times like that, when Sam forgets to be a cool dude and just speaks from the heart, I see the light in Sam's eyes when he talks to me about that girl and I see in his face the same intensity that Ben had when we were young. It takes my breath away and, sometimes, the memories engulf me. Ben, asking me to marry him, that fight we had and his passion when I tried to leave, and that weekend at his uncle's farm. Just the thought of that weekend brings me to my knees.

Of course, the memory of a far worse day—when Ben told me about his affair with Shelley—usually manages to eradicate those halcyon thoughts and swamp them under a layer of anguish and fury.

Today however, the tingling those memories stirred in me lingers and I think, "How long as it been since . . .?"

God, it's been weeks or even months since I last had a G.T., or "Good Time" as I used to call it. At some point, when I was in my twenties, my mom and I had one of those mother/daughter talks where she explained that masturbation was a sin. I was going through a period where I was quite the sensualist and fully enjoyed "making love to myself" and "releasing my inner Goddess" as I called it. I couldn't conceive of anything so bliss inducing and freeing to be a sin, and there was absolutely no way

I was going to give that up. Then, I met Ben and along came the kids and life in general, and now, 30 years later, there is always something more important to do than have a G.T.

Standing at the sink, staring down at the dripping mug in my hand I find myself wondering if it's possible that deep inside, part of me may have believed my mom. Because now, when I am as old, no, older, than my mother was then, it feels a little dirty and forbidden when I take the time to pleasure myself.

I made sure my daughter knew better and even went as far as giving her a book about masturbation. But lately, I haven't thought about it much and when I do I have a little spurt of shame and failure when I get out the "instant boyfriend" as my friend, Karen calls it.

Still, it is a Saturday afternoon and I do have the whole house to myself. Maybe it's time for a G.T. I make my way down to my bedroom, dig out the "instant boyfriend" from the bottom drawer of my dresser and throw it on the bed.

Keeping my eyes averted from the mirror on the dresser, (I have no desire to look at my naked body these days) I get undressed and pull down the sheets.

As I slide into bed, the crisp cotton sheets and a slightly lumpy mattress disappear and become a warm butter coloured dais draped with silk and satin fabrics. My stretch marks, dry skin, scars and other badges of honour from life as a mother and wife vanish into the ether. I am the nubile concubine of a desert sultan.

Some time ago, Beth had her friend Priya over and they started watching a Bollywood movie about the marriage of alliance between an emperor and a princess. I could not take my eyes off the television once the male star with his rugged good looks and fantastic body swaggered on-screen. The girls collapsed in giggles and soon turned it off, but that night, I watched all three and a half subtitled hours of it in my bedroom and he had been the hero of all my rare "Good Times" ever since.

As I sink into this tried and true—but still delicious fantasy—with my hot Bollywood sultan, my mind stills and meetings, car repairs, laundry, Ben, Shelley, even my kids fade like ice cubes beneath the hot desert sun.

Naked and unashamed, my alternate self stretches out her lithe body as she rests on a warm slab of marble under a canopy that protects her from the fierce desert sun. On the Persian rug below, she can see the legs and slippers of the two handmaids who massage sweet and spicy scented oils into her skin. Beyond the rug are the large yellow stone floor tiles that cover this massive square. We are in the courtyard of the desert palace of my sultan. Visible through the massive stone guard towers, is a wild desert terrain and beyond in the distance, rugged hills. It is an untamed and severe landscape and my ferocious warrior king is out patrolling the lands with his finest men. When he returns I am to be his prize.

He will be here soon and the handmaids are preparing me for him. The thought of his desire fills me with urgency; I cannot wait for him to come to me.

The servants help me sit up. While one gently affixes bracelets and anklets of bright ribbons and gold bangles to my light mocha coloured wrists and ankles, the other brushes my jet-black, long and thick hair - not a grey or mousy hair in sight. Again and again, the brush strokes through my hair, massaging my scalp and sending tingles all through my body. The other servant begins to stroke her hands up and down my calves and feet. I look down and see how intently she focuses on her actions as if my legs are the most important things in the world. Her strong fingers knead my arches, bringing a blissful sensation.

In the distance, I hear the sound of galloping hooves. My head spins as I intently search for the plumes of dust. There they are. In the lead on a beautiful black stallion, his powerful body moving fluidly on the surging beast rides my sultan. At the sight of him, desire shoots through me like lightning.

He doesn't even glance at the servants or his men as they race into the courtyard. His black eyes lock on mine, a fire lighting them from within. Smoothly he dismounts as the others ride on. Beside me, the servants gasp as he strides toward me, his boots ringing on the stone. They bow low and drift away like wisps of cloud leaving me alone before him.

Imperiously, his black eyes rake me from head to toe. He reaches out a black leather clad hand and seizes my chin, tilting my head so that I instinctively bend my neck, arching my breasts toward his gaze.

Wait a minute, that Bollywood star's eyes are a light green. Who is this guy?

My inner goddess, who has not been seen or heard from in years, raises her glorious face and roars at me, "Just go with it!" Where has she come from? I thought she was dead and buried along with my marriage and all my dreams.

Well, she may have been buried for years but she is definitely not dead. In fact, she is fierce, indomitable and determined that I pay attention. "Look at this glorious man. See how he wants you! *Look* at him!" It is a shout—a demand—and I obey.

The action in my G.T. fantasy has frozen as if someone has pressed the pause button. I "look" at my sultan. He is standing in front of my alternate self—feet braced apart, dark eyes narrowed from the bright sun.

My goddess is disgusted. "No, you imbecile. They're narrowed because of his blistering and primitive desire for you! He doesn't want *anyone* but you. He has ridden across the desert with the thought of you in his mind; he wants to *mate* with you! You, you, *you!*"

Mate? With *me?* I haven't mated with anyone in years, if ever. Have I ever "mated" with anyone? Even Ben?

My inner goddess has had enough. Through clenched teeth, she grinds out the words. "Just—go—with—it!" She turns on the action.

He strides up to the dais, puts his gloved hands on my waist and pulls me toward him. Instinctively, my legs part and circle his tall, strong frame, clasping him in an intimate embrace. He is damp from the ride and the heady scent of him fills my nostrils. My hands slide up his back and link around his neck, and I lift my head for his kiss.

His hands frame my face and his dark eyes bore into mine as he bends his head. His kiss starts out slow and deep but quickly turns hungry and urgent as our tongues carry out a sensuous battle.

In the background, I can hear the satisfied purr of my inner goddess.

His hands slide down my back and I lean into his touch,

my naked skin so sensitive against his gloved hands and his clothing. My legs grip him tightly and I hear his breath catch and feel a shudder shake his frame. He straightens suddenly, pulls my legs away and steps back.

Startled, I look up at his face and am infinitely relieved to see a wickedly sweet smile. With an economy of movement, he yanks at his gloves, pulling them off and tossing them away carelessly. "Undress me."

Oh, his voice. Deep and warm and so full of desire. With no sense of embarrassment, I slide off the marble dais eager to have him as naked as I.

First, I reach up and remove his headdress. His face, tight with desire, looks somehow younger and more approachable with his hair visible. The sight of him, without his headdress and the tasselled cord that holds it in place emphasizing his status, is something very few people are allowed to see. Knowing I am permitted in this inner circle causes a bubble of sheer happiness to explode inside me. Impishly, I ruffle his hair and am rewarded with a devastating smile and another searing kiss.

His powerful shoulders flex as I release the clasp holding his cloak and let it drop to the carpet. He ducks his head and lifts his arms to allow me to pull off his tunic and then I am clasped firmly against his naked chest. He is big and strong and undeniably male. My breasts swell, stimulated by his chest hair that rasps across the sensitive tips. His strong hands clench my buttocks and he pulls me up tight against his manhood and buries his face in my neck.

"Enough," he groans between kisses and nibbles on my neck. "I cannot wait much longer." He lifts me up to sit on the dais, gives me a hard kiss then steps away.

Swiftly, he kicks off his boots and removes his lower garments and then, he is as naked as I. In both my bedroom and in this wild desert location, my heart jerks and begins to pound.

Under his fierce gaze, my breasts tighten and pucker and, for a moment, I feel vulnerable and embarrassed. My inner goddess growls threateningly and suddenly unsure, my eyes flash up to his face. However, he is watching me with such a fiery passionate expression that my embarrassment melts away and I blossom like a flower in the sun. I relax and sink into his eyes, eager for him to continue.

His hands find my breasts and, this time, both my inner goddess and I groan with pleasure as he gently kneads them. He groans too, between clenched teeth as my hands slide down his washboard stomach and stroke his manhood, which jumps in my hand welcoming my touch. The intimate contact thrills us both and his hands slide down my body to pull me tight against him.

As I stroke him, his face changes, the angles harden as his desire intensifies and drives him forward. He can wait no longer. One hand rises to cup my shoulder and he eases me back on to the warm marble and follows me down until he is on top of me, supporting his upper body on his arms. He buries his face against my breasts and I am undone when he takes a hard, sensitive nipple into his mouth. My hands are buried in his hair, holding on to the only person I can while I whirl into a maelstrom of sensation.

"Are you ready?" he whispers. He has nibbled his way up to my face and ears. I writhe against him and my fingers dig into his shoulders. Oh, I am so ready for this.

His fingers find my innermost core and he strokes me. Shudders shake my frame and his body echoes the shudder. Pleasure builds inside of me until I cannot contain it.

"Take me!" Did I beg or demand? It doesn't matter.

"Look at me!"

My eyes lock on his as he positions himself. Beyond his head, the fabric of the tent rustles as a wild wind echoes our passion and beyond that is the desert castle, the bright blue, cloudless sky and the fiery, desert sun. And in this raw and wild moment with this glorious male, I understand what the goddess meant by "mating."

He leans forward, and strokes me again. My hips ride his hand but it is not enough and wordless, I beg him with my eyes and my body. He succumbs with a groan and slowly sinks into me.

Buried to the hilt, our bodies move together in the rhythm of the ages and the pleasure is almost unbearable. A heady sense of power and rightness sweeps through me as I cradle his unyielding dominant body against my soft, tender one and readily accept his thrusts. My arms embrace him just as his muscular arms wrap around me and clutch me tightly against his hard body.

And then, the most magnificent and freeing feeling that I have ever known sweeps through me. No thoughts now, just a vibrant, pulsing release that flows through my body saturating every cell like a dry sponge placed into fresh, clean and healthy water. It is beyond glorious and I lose myself in wave after way of feeling.

It is a while before I can stir and find myself back on

cotton sheets with the buzzing of the instant boyfriend in my ears. My hand is trembling as I reach down to turn it off. I lay in the bed, my body damp and sated and my mind fuzzy in the aftermath. What the heck was that? Have I ever felt such pleasure before?

Where did those thoughts and images come from? With a shaky laugh, I wipe my damp brow and let my arm flop down on the bed.

A little bubble of sadness bursts inside of me, as I realize that I am alone. It has been so long since someone loved me this way. So long since I felt that kind of connection.

And then, it hits me. It has been even longer since I felt that kind of connection with myself. When did I lose my love for myself? When did *I* stop loving *me*? A myriad of images flash through my mind, mother, protector of my children, wife, cuckolded wife, ex-wife, worker, friend, volunteer. So many hats. So many roles . . .

Somewhere under them was that sensuous woman who loved herself, took care of herself and allowed herself to feel intense pleasure—be it a cup of hot chocolate, the sight of the warm sun on spring flowers or the heady delight of loving her own body. I let her be buried under all the duties, disappointments and broken dreams and today, she broke out.

Tears fill my eyes and drip down my face. I had forgotten her, and like any plant ignored and uncared for she wilted. But, like a dog that loves its master no matter how foul the treatment, she loved me enough to come back and show me what I had lost.

I lay in bed for a long time, alone with my thoughts—something I haven't allowed myself for ages. I can feel the love of my inner goddesses soaking through me.

I didn't just have a G.T. today. I learned a very important lesson.

It is time to love myself again.

"I'm pretty sure that eating chocolate keeps wrinkles away because I have never seen a 10 year old with a Hershey bar and crows feet."

Amy Neftzger

CHOCOLATE

Who would question chocolate
with all its many uses?
Melted, grated, chopped or dipped
It stimulates the juices

The smell alone can stir the loins
The taste could do much more
So grab that hunk of chocolate
And watch your partner soar

Take a fruit, for instance
A strawberry or two
Melt dark chocolate in a pot
And plunge that fruit…yes, do.

Now share this treat in many ways
I leave to your devices
The chocolate will do its job,
As the senses it entices

So melt it, pour it, lick it off
Spread it in hollow places
I can almost guarantee
You'll be in her good graces

The Return
Cynthia Aston

He rose up out of the lake, shimmering, wet, fully erect. She lay there, legs spread, naked, unable to move. Her chest heaved, her large breasts spilling to the side. She tried to free herself but it was futile, her wrists and ankles held firmly by his minions. He was coming. Coming toward her, coming in her, coming all around her.

What surprised her most was that she didn't cry out. There was no cloth over her face, nothing stopping her from shouting, screaming. What surprised her most was that she was not afraid. She was hungry. She knew he couldn't hurt her, wouldn't. She knew he came because she called him, because she wanted him, she had wanted him forever.

Yet still she was unsure, uncertain. Did not expect to have anyone else around. Not these other creatures, these beautiful males and females, naked, powerful, silent.

He stopped at her feet, looming over her like a giant pine, dripping with lake, dripping with power, dripping with an earthy, gritty, love.

"You called me," he whispered. It was not a question.

She stared at him. His voice deep, rich, rising up from his groin, from the ground. The sound of his voice unleashed something and she cried out in ecstasy. "Whatever you want," he said, kneeling down at her feet. "Whatever you desire..."

He touched her bare foot, her left foot, and slowly began kneading it. She writhed in a pleasure she never knew. The deeper his fingers penetrated, the deeper her cries. Pain, pleasure, she couldn't tell them apart.

"Do you want me to stop?" he asked, his fingers softly sliding off.

"No!" she exclaimed. "Please, no."

The young man in the room wasn't sure what to do. He was a volunteer, trained in reflexology, foot massage. The patient, an older woman in her sixties, was in a coma. Her family wanted him there. Her family refused to believe she would not wake up.

But touching her feet, even as gently as he had, seemed to awaken something in the sleeping woman. Her body twitched, her hips moved, he could swear her hips had moved.

"That's highly unlikely," said the male nurse who adjusted knobs and wires. "Coma patients can't really feel anything. It's just your imagination."

The young man, in his late twenties, with dark curly hair, and olive skin, and green, green eyes, gazed at the woman after the nurse left the room.

"I don't believe him," he whispered, reaching for her feet again. "I think you know I'm here. I think you can feel me."

The sunlight glimmered on the lake. Birds sang in the tranquil woods. The male and female creatures holding her wrists and ankles let go. They knew she would not run.

Their master held her feet with so much love, with so much passion, she almost couldn't bare it. But she did, letting out a deep sigh, letting go, surrendering into the exquisite pleasure.

"You're going to awaken," said the young man in the room. "I know it. You're going to wake up."

Her family gathered around her in the early morning. It was her smile that made them gasp.

"Look!" whispered the youngest daughter. "Look! Mom is smiling!"

When she opened her eyes, the room shone with a light so beautiful, so tender, it brought tears to her eyes.

"You're back," whispered her husband, and he broke down, weeping.

"Yes," she whispered. "I'm back."

"Grow old along with me! The best is yet to be."

Robert Browning

"There is a fountain of youth: it is your mind, your talents, the creativity you bring to your life and the lives of people you love. When you learn to tap this source, you will truly have defeated age."

Sophia Loren

www.ingramcontent.com/pod-product-compliance
Lightning Source LLC
Chambersburg PA
CBHW060054260626
47160CB00005B/1671